MW01245411

SEEING RED
•
Dorothy P. O'Neill

AVALON BOOKS
NEW YORK

Published by Thomas Bouregy & Co., Inc.
160 Madison Avenue, New York, NY 10016

Library of Congress Cataloging-in-Publication Data

O'Neill, Dorothy P.
  Seeing red / Dorothy P. O'Neill.
       p. cm.
  ISBN 978-0-8034-9949-2 (acid-free paper)   1. Women—
Crimes against—Fiction.   2. Redheads—Fiction.   3. Serial
murders—New York (State)—New York—Fiction.
4. Murder—Investigation—Fiction.   I. Title.

 PS3565.N488S44   2009
 813'.54—dc22

                                                      2008048223

PRINTED IN THE UNITED STATES OF AMERICA
ON ACID-FREE PAPER
BY HADDON CRAFTSMEN, BLOOMSBURG, PENNSYLVANIA

SEEING RED
A Liz Rooney Mystery

To my writer friends, whose advice, inspiration and moral support I treasure:

Diane Lambright Berry, Pam Blackwood, Elizabeth DiMeo, Nancy Gotter Gates, Helen Goodman, Ellen Elizabeth Hinter and Dixie Land.

Prologue

In the Union Square subway station, around six-thirty, during Manhattan's evening rush hour, Justine Meister shouldered her way from the Lexington Avenue uptown express to the local and squeezed into a car before the doors slid shut. She'd be late getting home again tonight. On her way to the subway, she'd seen a darling little jacket in the window of a boutique.

And that reminded her—she hoped Otto wasn't still mad at her after their argument that morning. For the third month in a row, she'd run up his credit card bill so high, buying clothes, he could pay only the minimum. To avoid finance charges, Otto always liked to pay the full amount every month. That seemed silly. Why have a credit card if you had enough money to make the full payment?

Otto was so stubborn about owing money. After they were married, he'd paid off the balance on her credit card, canceled it, and put her on his. Now he was complaining, saying she was buying too many expensive clothes. He should have let her go on using her own card and paying the minimum. Daddy had never complained about that, or about bailing her out when she exceeded her limit, even after college, when he'd gotten her a job as receptionist in friend's firm. He and Mommy, too, understood she had to be well dressed, and her paycheck didn't cover Saks and Bergdorf's.

As she had many times lately, she felt a bit tearful. Everything had changed when she'd eloped with Otto. She hadn't taken her parents' ultimatum seriously: *"Break off with that man, or cut yourself off from us."*

The subway seemed even more jam-packed than usual tonight, she thought, and this spell of warm weather made it uncomfortably warm. Here it was, the first week of December, and it felt more like May. Instead of a heavy coat, she'd worn a cotton jacket to work. According to this morning's weather forecast, the unseasonable temperatures would hang around for another couple of days.

The train pulled into the next station. For a few seconds, the pressure of surrounding bodies eased as people got off, only to resume as more got on. During the influx, Justine felt a sudden stinging sensation in her left upper arm. Like the prick of a large pin, she thought. *Why would something like that be in her sleeve?* She puzzled over this for a minute or two before dismissing it from her mind, but after another few minutes she began to feel faint and found herself gasping for breath.

Two middle-aged women wedged next to her must have noticed. "Are you okay?" one asked.

"I feel . . . like . . . I'm going to black out," Justine managed to reply.

"Must be the heat," the other woman said. "You need some air. "You'd better get off at the next stop."

"That's my stop," the first woman said. "I'll help you up to the street and see that you get a taxi home."

At that moment the train pulled into the station. Justine heard herself murmuring her thanks as the woman guided her out of the car and toward the stairway. They'd just reached the street when her heart started racing, skipping, and pounding like a trip-hammer. Her knees gave way. She felt herself slumping. Just before she lost consciousness, she saw crowds of feet, some rushing past her, others slowing, surrounding her, and she heard the agitated voice of the woman who'd befriended her.

"Anyone with a phone, call 911!"

As she did every morning except Saturday and Sunday, Valerie Dawes stood in the crowd on the subway platform, awaiting her train. She checked her watch, thinking if it didn't come during the next few minutes, she'd be late getting to work—again. But old Dr. Feldman wouldn't give her a bad time about it today. He was going to a medical convention and wouldn't be in the office this morning.

Too bad the old man wasn't more like his son, she thought. Although the younger Dr. Feldman was a physical replica of his father—short, pudgy, balding, and all—he wouldn't be grumpy with her under any circumstances. They'd hit it off from the first day he'd joined his father's practice, last September. From day one, he'd insisted she call him Dr. Alvin. Soon, he'd suggested going for coffee after office hours, and then it was just Alvin. They'd been dating ever since, dining in upscale restaurants, viewing the best Broadway shows, partying with his friends.

Last Saturday night he'd taken her to dinner at the Tavern on the Green—grown a bit stodgy but still one of Manhattan's posh places, frequented mostly by wealthy tourists and baby boomers. Throw in the limo hired for the evening, and it all added up to a superimpressive date.

Shondra and Gina, with whom she shared a three-room apartment on East Twenty-eighth Street, had been impressed, too. "Wow, you'd better hang on to this one," Shondra had said, after hearing a full account the next morning.

Valerie had every intention of doing just that. Although Alvin's looks didn't qualify him as the man of her dreams, and there were no fireworks when he kissed her, the old man would be retiring next year, and Alvin would have the entire lucrative practice. If things continued to go as they had up till now, she could soon be the wife of a Park Avenue physician.

She knew the old man had sensed something going on between his son and his office nurse, and he'd made his disapproval clear to her. No *shiksa* for his Alvin. Back off, or she'd be out of a job.

Tough luck, Poppa. It's too late for that. After last night, she knew Alvin wasn't just having a fling.

With the sound of an approaching train, she felt herself caught up in a surge of people. Moving along in the crush, she felt something like a pinprick in her upper left arm. She must have left part of the price tag on this new blouse, she decided.

The train pulled in. She prepared herself for the usual jostling, but suddenly, before the doors opened, her heart started fluttering, she couldn't catch her breath, and she began to tremble all over.

"Help me . . . I think I'm going to faint," she heard herself saying, hoping someone in the crowd would hear her.

"Stand back! There's a woman taken ill here!" she heard a man's voice exclaim, just before she blacked out.

Chloe LaFleur's photo shoot ended on a sour note. It wasn't over till after six, and she'd expressed her annoyance to Bernie, the cameraman. It was his fault that the shoot had run so late. It certainly wasn't hers. She'd been a topflight model long enough to know all the right moves. Three times on the cover of *Vogue,* and Bernie had the gall to tell her she hadn't looked good in most of the shots.

On the elevator, she checked her watch. It would be almost six-thirty when she got down to the street. Try to get a cab in Manhattan at that hour. She'd have to take the subway home, and by the time she showered and changed clothes, she'd be very late meeting Giles for dinner at the St. Regis. She liked to arrive a few minutes late for all her dates to make sure she wasn't the one kept waiting. Besides being humiliating, getting there first implied eagerness. Eager as she was to spend this evening with Giles, she'd planned to show up a bit late, as usual—but not late enough to annoy him.

She glanced at her watch. Chances were, he was already on his way to the St. Regis. She pictured him being escorted by the maître d' to the table held in reserve for Sinclair family members. Even if she reached him by cell phone to explain, how would he react to such a long wait?

Giles was a recent addition to her roster of male admirers, and by far the most qualified. Besides being handsome, well-educated, and urbane, he had the unmistakable aura of old money about him. If she played it right, a chunk of that money would go for a two-carat diamond engagement ring, and she could say bye-bye to the career she'd once thought would be glamorous and the Gramercy Park apartment she could barely afford.

But she'd be kidding herself if she didn't face the fact that there were other women with same idea, she thought, as she hurried toward the subway. She knew it wasn't likely that any one of them could even come close to her in looks, but a woman in his own social circle might have the advantage—some horse-faced, high-society babe whose father had prepped with Giles' father, and whose mother had made her social debut with his mother. A little hick-town nobody, no matter how beautiful, might lose out.

Meanwhile, she'd continue seeing Eddie and Marco.

They both wanted to marry her. If Giles hadn't come into the picture, she'd have been satisfied with either one. Back in Bronson's Corners, they'd both have been considered good catches.

As she joined the crowd descending the subway stairs, Chloe told herself she was lucky that, so far, she'd been able to keep each of the three men from finding out she was seeing the others. Juggling dates wasn't easy, but she wasn't ready to give any of them up. It would be awkward if one of them found out he wasn't the only one. And she knew there'd be trouble with Marco. She'd discovered he had a jealous nature and a hot temper one evening at a popular after-theatre spot, when a man at a nearby table had given her too much of a once-over.

To her dismay, she just missed a train. While she waited for the next one, the empty platform gradually became jam-packed. Wedged into the crowd, she felt a jab in her right arm. Someone must be carrying a sharp object, she thought.

The train pulled in. Moments after she boarded, she noticed that the car was so stuffy, she found it hard to breathe. Must be the warm weather yesterday and today, she decided. Only a few weeks till Christmas, but it felt more like Memorial Day.

Suddenly, she found herself gasping. At the same time, her heart started fluttering, and she felt as if her knees had turned to jelly.

Voices, a man and a woman's, sounded from the crowd around her.

Dorothy P. O'Neill

"Are you all right, miss?"

"She's not all right—she looks like she's going to faint."

That was the last voice Chloe would ever hear.

Chapter One

Liz Rooney's eyes widened as she stared at her boss, Medical Examiner Dan Switrzer. "Three young women, *dead,* after fainting in the subway—all during the past twenty-four hours?" she asked.

"That's right, Lizzie," Dan replied. "Two of them DOA when the paramedics arrived. The third one died in the ambulance."

Dan must suspect foul play, or he wouldn't have come to her desk first thing in the morning to tell her about this, Liz thought. How lucky she was to be working for her father's closest friend. Like Pop, a retired NYPD homicide detective, Dan always went along with her penchant for following sensational murders. The two of them had been encouraging this interest since her red hair had been in pigtails. They'd watched it develop into full-blown amateur sleuthing, now an important aspect of her life.

Now, with Pop and Mom relocated to Florida, Dan had become a proxy parent. The information he provided, added to what the man in her life, NYPD detective "Ike" Eichle, was willing to divulge, kept her passion for solving homicides going.

"I get the feeling you think all three of them were murdered," she said.

"They were all young and pretty and appeared to be in excellent health," Dan replied. "And I was told all three passed out during rush hours in same area of the Lexington local. Too much similarity for coincidence."

"How could someone get away with murder on a crowded subway with so many potential witnesses?"

"We think it was done by lethal injection. That way it could have gone unnoticed. In the preliminary examinations, fresh needle marks showed up on the arms of all three victims."

Liz pondered this. "I can see how that might work," she said, "But this is flu-shot season. Couldn't that explain the needle marks?"

"It could, except all three victims showed signs of cyanide poisoning."

"Cyanide!" Liz exclaimed. "I thought that was a poisonous gas."

"There are various forms of cyanide," Dan replied. "If a liquid form is injected, it induces death within a very short time."

"Wouldn't it be hard to stick a needle through layers of clothing?"

"It's been unseasonably warm for the past couple of

days. Most likely those women were wearing light-weight clothing."

Liz nodded. "For the past two days I've been wearing a sweater instead of a jacket." Still not convinced, she added, "But thousands of young women ride that subway line every day. Couldn't three out of those thousands have had heart attacks or something?"

Dan shook his head. "Besides the signs of cyanide in the systems of all three victims, there are too many other parallels. I'm not ruling out homicide till all the autopsies are complete."

His eyes held a serious expression as he added, "And here's a parallel I didn't mention. You'll identify with this one, Lizzie. All three women are redheads."

"Oh!" Liz raised a hand to touch her own hair. "That *does* sound like homicide. Someone has it in for redheaded women. This is horrible."

"We could be talking about a serial killer," Dan replied. He paused, as if he were weighing his next words. "You take the Lexington Avenue local and the Thirty-fourth Street crosstown bus to and from work, don't you? And your usual subway stations are Twenty-eighth Street and Thirty-third Street, right?"

"I usually walk to the bus, but, yes, I take the subway to and from those stations when the weather's bad. Are you saying that's where . . . ?"

He nodded. "According to paramedics' reports, all the victims collapsed during morning and evening rush hours, between the Union Square and Thirty-third Street stations."

She stared at him, speechless, for a moment. "It was

raining this morning. I could have been one of those women," she said, shuddering at the thought of a poisoned needle being jabbed into her arm.

But the possibility of matching wits with Ike on this one lightened her grim feelings. This would be the first case of a serial killer they'd ever come up against together.

Discussing homicides was an important facet of her relationship with Ike. It hadn't always been that way. Less than a year ago, Ike had strongly disapproved of her interest in murder cases and made no attempt to hide his resentment when she showed up at crime scenes with Dan. She and her best friend since first grade, NYPD officer Sophie Pulaski, had dubbed Ike "Detective Sourpuss."

Ike's attitude had changed when she'd happened upon a clue that helped him solve a case, and the DA acknowledged her input. After that, things between her and Detective Sourpuss had gone from chilly to chummy, then on to much deeper feelings. Now they were planning a February wedding.

Dan's voice came into her thoughts. "I've put the three bodies on priority, and I expect to have the full autopsy reports sometime tonight." He cast her a look of concern. "But, while we're waiting for the results, to be on the safe side, I'll spring for a cab to get you home tonight and to work tomorrow."

"Oh, thanks, Dan, but that's not necessary. Even if it's raining, I can walk to and from the bus stop."

Dan shook his head. "I don't want you anywhere near those subway stations. If the autopsies show what

I believe they will, I'll phone you tonight and let you know, so you can take a cab in the morning."

"I could ride the subway if I wore a scarf over my head, or a hat," Liz persisted. She recalled how she'd tried to avoid pursuit by reporters after a recent adventure had thrust her into the limelight. "You know I'm getting pretty good at disguises."

"But this time you wouldn't just be trying to throw newshounds off the track," Dan said, as he turned to go.

She appreciated his concern, but he was being over-protective, she thought. If tomorrow was rainy, she felt sure she'd be safe on the subway with her head well covered. There was no need for Dan to pay cab fare.

Shortly before quitting time, Ike called, saying he'd just been talking to Dan. "I phoned him concerning an unrelated autopsy, and he told me about the subway deaths. Lou and I have been away from the station house since early morning, and we hadn't heard."

"I guess Dan told you he believes the deaths are homicides," Liz said.

"More than that," Ike replied. "Dan said he thinks there's a serial killer out there, and after he told me all three victims are redheads, I think so, too. I'm going to pick you up and drive you home, so stay put."

His voice, almost gruff, disclosed his concern for her. She pictured him swiping at a stray lock of his sandy hair—a frequent gesture when something was plaguing him. She knew there'd be a serious expression in his hazel eyes, and his ruggedly handsome face would be etched with worry. It would be useless to tell him she could walk home from the bus. Besides, she loved feeling cared about and looked after by him.

"I'll be a little late, but I'll get there as soon as I can," he continued. "Will you wait for me at the main entrance?"

"I'll be there," she replied.

A few minutes later, Sophie phoned from her squad car, saying she was parked outside a doughnut shop, waiting for her partner to get coffee for them. For a while Liz had wondered if the close relationship she and Sophie had maintained since first grade would change now that Sophie was newly married to fellow NYPD officer Ralph Perillo. It hadn't.

From the tone of Sophie's voice, Liz felt sure she'd heard about the three subway deaths. "Hi, Liz. I'm glad I caught you before you left for home."

"I guess you know about the women on the subway."

"Yeah—it's all over the station house. What did Dan say about it? Any chance they're homicides?"

Sophie wouldn't have asked that question if she knew all three women had red hair, Liz thought. That would have alerted her to the possibility of a serial killer, and she'd be all fired up about it. Evidently the buzz around the station house hadn't included the hair color information.

"Dan's almost sure the subway deaths were homicides," she replied, "and here's why . . ."

Sophie listened, then gasped. "Wow! Looks like someone's out to get every good-looking, young red-headed woman he happens to see. And he's operating during rush hours on the six train. I don't have to tell you this makes you a target, Liz."

"I know," Liz said, "But . . ."

Sophie broke in. "Have you talked to Ike? Does he know?"

"Yes, he's picking me up here in a little while. And Dan's going to let me know what shows up in the autopsies. If these are homicides, and it's raining tomorrow, I'll make sure my hair's covered when I take the subway to the bus. Dan said I should take a cab, but—"

"Are you crazy? Don't even think of taking the subway!" Sophie exclaimed. "It sounds like the killer rides the six regularly during rush hours. He could have noticed you already and decided you're next. He'd know you're a redhead. Your wearing a hat or a scarf isn't going to stop him."

"Okay, okay!" Liz replied with a laugh. "Even if it's pouring tomorrow, I'll walk to the bus."

Sophie laughed, too. "Wouldn't this be a great case for Pulaski and Rooney?" she asked, referring to their dream plan of someday becoming private investigators. She'd told Liz if that ever happened, she was going to keep *Pulaski* in there, but she'd be Perillo everywhere else.

Liz nodded, thinking of her grandmother on Staten Island, from whom she was sure she'd inherited her penchant for following homicide cases, as well as her red hair. Regular visits to Nick's Crowning Glory kept Gram's hair red, and Liz's sleuthing kept Gram's own interest in murder cases going. More than once, Gram's observations had helped Liz dig up clues. If the PI dream ever materialized, Liz and Sophie intended to make Gram a part of it.

Sophie must have had the same thought. "Your Gram would love to be in on this one," she said.

As usual, whenever they talked about Pulaski and Rooney, Private Investigators, Liz's imagination took off. "Gram would probably insist on being a decoy," she said.

As always, Sophie went along with the flight of fancy. "Yeah—she'd keep her eyes open so she could identify someone close to her in the crowd, and she'd wear thick bandages on her arms so the needle couldn't get through."

"Only one thing wrong with that," Liz said. "Gram's hair is as red as it ever was, but she's seventy-four, and the killer has been going after young women."

"No problem," Sophie replied. "There could have been a mean, older redheaded woman who made the killer's childhood miserable—a teacher, or a stepmother, maybe—and over the years he developed a psychosis, and now he's getting even."

"Then why is he going after *young* redheads?" Liz asked. A moment later she thought of an answer. "I know," she said. "He figures all redheads are mean at heart, and . . ."

"And the young ones will eventually get to be exactly like that older woman who made his life a living hell," Sophie declared. In the next breath she said Mike was there with the coffee. "I'll phone you tomorrow. Meanwhile, be careful."

She would, Liz resolved. She wasn't going to take any chances on becoming the next red-haired subway victim, even if she had to walk to and from the bus in the rain every day until the killer was caught.

Chapter Two

Ike braked his Taurus near the entrance to Liz's building. "Will the day ever come when I don't have to worry about you?" he asked, as she got in. He followed up with a light kiss, adding, "Sorry to sound so cranky, but I'm just getting over your last scrape, and now this."

"Well, excuse me for having red hair," she replied, her voice slightly edgy.

The frown on his face melted into a grin. "Don't get your Irish up," he said, turning the Taurus into the stream of traffic. "If you weren't the love of my life, I could take a more objective view of some nut's riding the six train, inoculating redheaded beauties with poisoned needles."

"... *love of my life ... beauties ...*" Ike seldom came out with such blarney. She smiled. "Are you sure there's not a touch of Irish somewhere among the Eichles in your Germanic background?"

18

"Come to think of it, there was a Michael McEichle," he replied.

She laughed. "Just like there was a Ludwig Von Rooney in *my* background."

They were bantering to lessen their concern about the subway deaths, she thought. "There's no proof of foul play yet," she said. "Dan's going to phone me tonight with the results. If I take the subway tomorrow, maybe I won't have to wear a scarf or a turban, after all."

She wasn't surprised when his reaction to this statement was much the same as Sophie's. "If the autopsies show those deaths were homicides, don't even think about taking the subway. Even with your hair covered, it would be too risky. You have a redhead's eyes and complexion. Hiding your hair would only attract the killer's attention."

He was right, she thought. Blue eyes, light eyebrows, fair skin, and a scarf over her head could suggest hidden red hair.

Ike looked pensive. "With their hair covered or not, redheads might not be safe anywhere in the vicinity of those subway stops," he said. "Couldn't you do something to change the color of your hair? That way you could let it all hang loose."

"Dye my hair . . . ?" Liz pondered this. She knew there were products that darkened hair and gradually washed out. "Sure, I could do that," she replied. "The color would fade a little every time I washed my hair, but if the killer isn't caught by time the red starts showing, I could do it again."

He nodded. "Sounds good. I wouldn't want you to

go brunet permanently. I have my heart set on a red-headed wife."

They exchanged smiles. He was getting pretty good with the sweet talk, she thought.

She saw him check his watch. "Do you have dinner planned, or shall we go somewhere?" he asked.

"I want to be home when Dan phones, so we'd better eat in," she replied. "I'll fix hamburgers and a salad."

He nodded. "Okay. We'll stop at that big drugstore at the corner of Second and Twenty-third and get your hair stuff. If Dan says the deaths were homicides, you can go brunet tonight."

"Or if he says they died of natural causes, I'll return the dye to the store tomorrow," she replied.

Ike maneuvered the car into a parking space near the converted brownstone where Liz lived, on the fringes of Gramercy Park. The one-room-with-kitchenette-and-bath walk-up (which landlady Rosa Moscaretti referred to as "a studio apartment"), had been home to her ever since Pop and Mom had sold the Staten Island house and moved to Florida.

"It'll be great when the Taurus can stay parked here all night, every night," Ike said, pocketing the car keys.

Liz cast him a knowing smile. What he actually meant was it would be great when *he* could stay parked with *her,* all night, every night.

She was one of two tenants in Rosa and Joe Moscaretti's brownstone. She'd formed a close relationship with the Moscarettis, which included constant vigilance by the motherly Rosa, and Joe, a Marine Corps veteran. Nothing got by those two. It was as if she'd become a substitute for their daughter, now married and living in California. At times she felt as if she were a teenager again, back living with Pop and Mom.

But that would change when she and Ike were married. She gave him a light kiss. "In a few weeks, you and the Taurus will have permanent spaces around here," she said. "And yours won't be in my dinky little place," she added, reminding him that Mr. Klein, the other tenant, would be moving out of the larger apartment in advance of their wedding, and the Moscarettis had offered it to them.

They'd jumped at it, of course. *Living room, bedroom, big kitchen, and a small extra room that could double as quarters for visiting parents and Ike's computer.* With both Ike's place and hers too small, they'd been looking for a larger apartment in which to start their married life. Liz, who slept on a sofa bed in the middle of her one room, and whose sink, stove, and fridge were wedged along one wall behind a screen, wanted a real bedroom and kitchen. Now they could have it all.

"We'll have more room than my apartment and yours put together," Ike said.

On their way up the steps to the brownstone's entrance, they saw Rosa at her window. She waved, and by the time they entered the building, she was waiting for them in the hall outside her apartment.

"Hello, dearie—hello, Ike," she said with her usual

welcoming smile. "I've been watching for you. I'm making chicken cannellonis, and there'll be more than enough for you if you'd like them."

Liz knew she spoke for Ike, too, when she replied, "Oh, Rosa, thank you. We'd love them." She suspected he was thinking that Rosa's chicken cannellonis had it all over hamburgers. Besides her fondness for Rosa and Joe, Rosa's frequent willingness to share her wonderful Italian cooking was another reason to be thankful she could continue living upstairs from them.

"Soon as the cannellonis are done, I'll send Joe up with them," Rosa said.

"Do you think there'll be anything on the news yet about the redheads on the subway?" Liz asked, when they entered her apartment.

Ike shook his head. "As things stand, maybe not, but if those autopsies show the deaths were homicides, it could be on TV and in the newspapers first thing tomorrow." He cast her a grin. "Joe might insist on escorting you to work. You might find yourself with an ex-Marine bodyguard."

With a laugh, she wagged the bag containing the hair color. "I won't need a bodyguard or anything else if I have to use this tonight," she said.

"You'd better count on using it," he replied. "The more I think about those three deaths . . ." He paused, turning the TV to a news channel. "Let's stay tuned just in case the news breaks before Dan has a chance to phone you."

Like Dan, Ike believed the subway deaths were the work of a serial killer, Liz thought.

She noticed him glancing at her gateleg table with a slight frown. "I'll set up that contraption for dinner," he said.

Liz watched him struggle with the old table Gram had given to her. It had always been hard to set up. In her pre-Ike days, she'd seldom used it. She'd taken microwaved frozen dinners to the sofa.

"I'll be glad when we can eat at a regular table," he growled, prodding at a balky leg.

She nodded. "Me, too. I wish we could keep it un-folded all the time, but in this small space, we'd be bumping into it whenever we turned around."

"Well, when we're settled in the other apartment, we can keep it folded up all the time, with a lamp on it, or something," he replied, tugging the second leaf into place.

She nodded, smiling. "While we dine at a nice, big table in the alcove off our nice, big kitchen."

"We should toast that thought," Ike said, heading for the kitchen shelf Liz referred to as the wine rack.

While he opened a bottle of Chianti, she brought two goblets down from her dish cabinet. They'd taken their first sips when a knock sounded on the door, followed by Joe's voice.

"Moscarettis' dinner delivery!"

All during the meal, Liz found herself on the alert for Dan's phone call. It didn't come, nor did any television

news about the subway deaths materialize. They finished eating, cleared the table, and settled on the sofa
with coffee.

"I can tell you're itching to get your teeth into this
case," Ike said. "But until we know for sure what's what,
there's not much to discuss. Sure, it happened in my
precinct, but even if it turns out to be homicide, Lou and
I might not be put on the case."

*Three murders that looked like the work of a serial
killer.* Chances were slim of this being assigned to anyone else on the squad, Liz thought. Before Pop retired,
he'd worked with Ike for a while. "He's the best young
detective to join the squad since I was a rookie," Pop
had told her. The close friendship between the two of
them was one of the joys of her life.

"While we're waiting to know what's what, let's suppose the three deaths are established as murders and
you're on the case," she said. "How would you start your
investigation?"

"Pretty much routine," he replied. "Interviews with
people who knew the women, starting with husbands
and boyfriends."

Liz nodded. During her sleuthing, she'd learned
that husbands or boyfriends of women murder victims
were the first to be considered possible suspects—or,
according to current terminology, persons of interest.
*But if, as it now appeared, the same person had killed
all three women, wouldn't that rule out these husbands
or boyfriends?*

"Assuming one of these husbands or boyfriends
wanted his red-haired wife or girlfriend dead, so he

jabbed her with a poisoned needle," she said, "why would he go on a spree afterward to kill other redheads? It doesn't make sense."

Suddenly, she recalled her phone conversation with Sophie. "I talked with Sophie about this, and she suggested that maybe a redheaded woman in the killer's past made his life a living hell, and now he's getting even."

"That's definitely something to consider," Ike said. He flashed a grin. "But a red-haired woman wouldn't have to be in the killer's past to make him want to rid the world of redheads. She could have been making his life hell right up till the day he decided to do it." Quickly, he drew her close with a kiss. "But *my* redhead has done exactly the opposite," he added.

Liz stared at him in pleased surprise. *That was just short of calling her an angel!*

The phone rang at that moment. She reached for it, saying, "I hope this is Dan."

It was.

"Lizzie," he said, "it's just as I thought. All three autopsies showed toxic substances, including cyanide. We definitely have three homicides here."

Chapter Three

Seeing her reflection in the bathroom mirror the next morning was much more of a shock than it had been the night before. In the mellow glow of a seventy-five-watt bulb, her new, warm, brown hair color had lived up to the name on the box—Sultry Sable. Now, in the pallid, early-morning light coming through the window, the color looked dark enough to be named Murky Mink.

The contrast blanched her skin and faded her eyebrows and lashes. It accentuated her freckles, which now stood out like angry, miniature polka dots. A little makeup would solve those problems, but there was nothing she could do about the hair color. She'd have to live with it as long as necessary.

On the plus side, however, her eyes seemed to be a brighter blue, and, most important, nobody would ever guess she was a redhead. She could take the subway without wondering if her next stop would be the morgue.

Although she'd turned the TV on as soon as she'd woken up, there'd been nothing on the news about the subway homicides. Maybe there'd been some delay in notifying all three victims' families that the deaths were not from natural causes. How awful for those families, she thought. It was bad enough for them to know their loved ones had died on the subway and been taken to the city morgue—but to be told they'd been murdered would be devastating.

The killing of three, young, red-haired women on the Manhattan subway would be sensational news, she thought. Unlike drug-related murders and others considered too commonplace to warrant anything but local coverage, this story would be all over national TV. She should phone Pop and Mom before the news broke and let them in on everything.

Mom answered with a sleepy voice. "Liz—it's so early, dear—we're not up yet. Is everything all right? Are you okay?"

She heard Pop in the background, saying something.

"Everything's okay, Mom," she said. "Tell Pop I'm fine, but I need to talk with both of you."

"I'll tell him to get on the extension," Mom said.

She knew telling them would be upsetting, so she decided to begin by announcing that she'd colored her hair, then follow up with the reason for it. The strategy worked well.

"Thanks for letting us know," Pop said. "I hope this

killer can be caught before he strikes again. Clever of Ike, getting you to dye your hair."

Mom broke in with a sigh. "Your beautiful red hair. Are you sure the dye will wash out?"

"I hope so," she replied, recalling her earlier dissatisfaction.

But a final look into the bathroom mirror before leaving for work left her pleasantly surprised. Like the mellow lightbulb last night, sunshine streaming through the window softened her hair color. She stood there gazing at it for a few minutes. *Not bad at all.* If she didn't know that Ike liked her red hair, Sultry Sable might be a keeper.

The TV weather channel forecast another day of mild, almost springlike temperatures. She put on the same light sweater she'd worn the day before. On her way to the door, she switched the TV to a news channel for one last check, but there was still no mention of the subway homicides. It might come on any minute now, she thought, turning the set off. She decided to stop in at the Moscarettis' and let them know about it beforehand. It was almost eight. Rosa would be in the kitchen, cooking breakfast.

When she knocked on their door, she heard Rosa call out, "Joe, will you see who that is?"

Joe's voice filtered through the door. "It can't be anyone for us. We would have heard the buzzer. Someone's looking for Liz or Mr. Klein, and they came to the wrong apartment."

"Who'd be coming to see Liz or Mr. Klein at this hour?" Rosa asked.

Joe opened the door. He stared at Liz for a moment, his face blank. "I think you got the wrong apartment, miss," he said. "If you're looking for Liz Rooney or Mortimer Klein, they're upstairs."

Score one for Sultry Sable!

She laughed. "Joe, it's me, Liz. I need to talk to you and Rosa."

"Liz?" he asked, in disbelief. He gave her another stare. "What happened to your hair?"

"I dyed it. That's why I need to talk to you and Rosa."

At last, he smiled, saying, "You have some explaining to do." He swung the door open wide, calling, "Rosa, you gotta see this."

"Gotta see what?" Rosa called back. "And who was at the door?"

"It's Liz. She has a surprise for you."

Rosa appeared, her welcoming smile fading into a look of startled incredulity. "Oh. My God, dearie, what have you done to your hair?"

Liz launched into the explanation. When she finished, both Rosa and Joe expressed their feelings concerning the three murders.

"It's just terrible," Rosa said. "There should be cops on all the trains till the killer is caught."

Joe was all for organizing a force of subway vigilantes.

Rosa gave her a hug. "Thanks for letting us know. If you didn't, and we heard it on TV, we'd have been worried sick." She paused, eyeing Liz's hair with a slight frown. "You look so different. . . ."

"I like it," Joe said. "She almost looks Italian."

Rosa glanced toward the kitchen. "Coffee's ready. Can you sit down and have a cup with us, dearie?"

"You know I'd love to, but I should be getting to work," Liz replied.

Rosa gave her a good-bye hug. "Let's hope the killer doesn't go after another red-haired girl today," she said. "But if he does, at least it won't be you."

Liz decided to take the subway instead of walking. With the weather unseasonably warm again today, women wouldn't be wearing heavy coats. And with no news of the killings to warn them, women with red hair wouldn't hide their hair under hats or scarves, or camouflage it, as she'd done. To the killer, the sight of one redhead in the crowd could be like a bright crimson flag to a bull. If she kept her eyes open, possibly she could head off another homicide.

Before today, she'd never taken particular notice of anyone in the subway. Now, as she joined the crowd waiting for the train, she looked carefully at everyone in sight. She didn't expect to see someone brandishing a hypodermic needle—the killer wouldn't be so obvious—but if she glimpsed a red-haired woman, she'd get to her as quickly as possible and warn her.

When the train pulled into the station, she hadn't spotted any redheads. After she boarded, she kept alert but didn't see one in the car, either. She hoped the same held true for other cars.

She got off at her stop, her eyes searching the crowd for signs that something had happened in one of the other cars. She saw and heard nothing unusual. If a red-haired woman was in one of the other cars, evidently the killer wasn't. But with the many hundreds of riders using this line during rush hours, both victim and killer could be anywhere along the route. With a sigh, she told herself that her chances of preventing another homicide were next to zero, but she'd done what she could.

Walking to catch the crosstown bus, she decided to call Gram. News of the subway homicides would be breaking soon, if it hadn't already, she thought, taking her phone out of her purse. She hoped it hadn't.

The instant Gram answered, Liz knew from her agitated voice that the news has broken on TV. "Oh, Liz dear, I'm thankful you called. I just heard the terrible news about those three red-haired women murdered on the subway. I've been so worried about you. . . ."

"No need to worry," Liz replied. "I'm not—"

Gram broke in. "No need for me to worry about you when there's a maniac killing red-haired girls on the same subway you take every day?"

"Not every day, Gram, and, anyway, I'm not a redhead anymore. Ike suggested I dye my hair, and I did."

As far as Gram was concerned, Ike could do no wrong, and this was further proof. "Oh, God bless him," she said.

"Yes, it was a good idea," Liz replied. "No one would take me for a redhead now. My hair's brown."

"Are you sure there's no red showing?" Gram asked. "It didn't turn out looking dark auburn? That might qualify as red to the killer."

"Absolutely no trace of red," Liz assured her.

"Well, now that my mind's at ease, there's something

I want to tell you," Gram said. "I know you must be on your way to work. Can you talk for a few minutes?"

"Sure, Gram—what's on your mind?"

"I'm getting a new cat," Gram replied.

Liz felt surprised and pleased. She knew Gram still missed big, black Hercules, who'd died a couple of years before at the ripe old age of nineteen. At the time, Gram had stated that she wouldn't get another cat. "I could never find one like Hercules," she'd said. "He was one of a kind."

"Oh, Gram, I think that's great," Liz said. She'd loved Hercules, too. Every day, after classes were dismissed at Our Lady Queen of Peace School on Staten Island, she'd always gone to Gram's house, a short walk from the school, off New Dorp Lane, and waited for Mom to pick her up on the way home from work. Hercules had seemed to know when school was out. He'd be in Gram's front window when she came up the street—watching for her, she was convinced. By the time she was on Gram's porch, he'd be at the door, waiting to circle her legs, sounding a throaty greeting—a combination of a meow and a loud purr.

"What made you change your mind, Gram?" she asked.

"I was clearing out the storeroom in the basement, and I came across the cat carrier. I thought I'd gotten rid of it, but there it was. It got me thinking about Hercules and what good company he was, especially after your grandfather died, and the first thing I knew, I'd decided to get another cat."

"When are you getting him?" Liz asked.

"I'm going to take my time. I've waited this long, so I might as well get what I want. I checked with the animal shelter, but no luck. I want a black male kitten who looks as much like Hercules as possible. No white paws or other prominent white markings."

Liz recalled that Hercules had a small white spot on his chest. "Are you going to hold out for that little speck of white?" she asked.

Gram laughed. "No. I have to be realistic. But who knows? Maybe I'll find a black kitten with white on his chest."

"There's gotta be one out there somewhere," Liz said. "Maybe next time you go to the animal shelter, you'll find him."

Gram's announcement had stirred up many memories. After they said good-bye, and when she boarded the bus, Liz continued to think of old Hercules.

The bus looked full, but she found a seat toward the rear, next to an elderly Asian man. With Hercules still on her mind, she found herself smiling, recalling how she'd learned to imitate his throaty *mmmerrrow.* Gram used to say she couldn't tell whether it was her cat or her granddaughter. It had been years since she'd vocalized like that. Could she still do it? On an impulse, she tried out her long-ago expertise, keeping it soft and low.

"Mmmerrrow!"

Apparently it wasn't soft and low enough. Heads turned. The Asian man cast a startled look at her handbag.

She knew Ike would get a laugh out of this when she told him. She could barely keep from laughing out loud herself. When she got off the bus at her stop, the humor of it still lingered. For a little while, childhood memories had crowded thoughts of the subway homicides from her mind, but now they returned, along with a grim question.

Would another red-haired woman be brought into the morgue today?

Chapter Four

On the way to her workstation, Liz glanced into Dan's office. Although he generally got to his desk earlier than she, he wasn't there. She'd have to wait awhile to show off her new hair.

When he'd phoned last night with the autopsy results, she'd assured him he needn't worry about her becoming subway victim number four. "By tomorrow I'll be sporting brown hair," she'd told him.

"Well, I guess that should work," he'd replied. He didn't sound totally convinced, she'd thought. Like Gram, he feared there'd be russet glints to betray her. Too bad he wasn't at his desk to see the startling transformation.

Before starting work, she turned on her desk TV. The subway homicides were all over the news. This morning's bulletin hadn't been broadcast in time to warn all work-bound redheads, but those who'd gotten wind of it must be in a panic. Just as she was wondering if the killer had struck again that morning, she saw Dan going toward his office. He paused, glanced her way, and broke into a broad smile.

"I almost didn't recognize you, Lizzie," he called. "The hair looks good."

A few minutes later, Sophie phoned. "No buzz about another subway homicide during this morning's rush hour," she said. "Looks like the killer's lying low till this evening. Did you walk to the bus or take a cab to work?"

Liz couldn't resist teasing her. "No. I took the subway to the bus stop, and I didn't even cover my hair."

Sophie's response crackled over the wire. "Are you off your rocker? Why in the world did you take a chance like that? When we talked yesterday, you said—"

Liz laughed. "Simmer down. Last night I dyed my hair brown."

"You did *what?*"

"That's right. I'm not a redhead anymore—at least not for about three weeks. It'll gradually wash out."

"That was good thinking, but what's Ike going to say about it?"

"Ike came up with the idea, but he hasn't seen the results yet."

"I can't picture you without . . ." Sophie began, then, "I gotta go," she said. "I'll phone you tomorrow."

Ike called a few minutes afterward. "How'd your hair turn out?" he asked.

"It's perfect," she replied. "No one would ever guess I'm anything but sultry sable brown."

Ike's chuckle came over the wire. " 'Sultry sable brown'? Hey, I like the sound of that!"

If there'd been another red-haired woman killed on the Lexington Avenue local this morning, wouldn't Ike know about it, and wouldn't he have told her right away, instead of asking how the dye job turned out?

His next words convinced her there'd been no further subway homicides. "I wish I didn't have to wait till tonight to check out your new look. I'll see you at your place, but I'll be a little late. I'll pick up some takeout. How about Mexican?"

"You look so different," Ike said, moments after she opened the door. "For a second, I thought I was kissing somebody else."

"But it was the same old Liz kiss," she replied.

"The same *wonderful* Liz kiss," he corrected, on his way to the kitchenette with the takeout.

Day by day, he was getting better and better at sweet talk!

She'd already set up the gateleg table. Now she brought out china plates, something Ike had once considered unnecessary when they were having takeout. Early in their relationship, he'd told her he always ate takeout straight from the cartons, while lolling in his recliner.

Now, watching her set the table, he warned, "You'll probably have to break me of a few more bachelor habits."

"I had some sloppy habits of my own before you came into my life," she admitted. "I used to eat microwaved frozen dinners out of the box, while sitting on the sofa."

He looked surprised. "You did? But the first time I

dropped in with takeout, you set the table with dishes and everything."

"I wanted to impress you."

"You didn't need a table with a lace cloth and dishes to impress me. I was hooked on you long before we ever ate together."

"Even while we were calling each other by our last names, and you made it clear you disapproved of my amateur sleuthing?"

He laughed. "Even then."

She smiled, thinking how things had changed since then. Now, the DA acknowledged her input, and Ike let her in on almost everything.

"So, how was your day?" he asked, when they were seated at the table. "Any word from your folks, or Gram?"

"Gram called. She's looking for a new cat. Remember, I told you about the black cat she used to have and how I could imitate his meowing?"

"Yeah. Hercules, right?"

"Right, and wait till you hear this. . . ." She told him about the incident on the bus.

"I wish I could have been there," he replied, after a hearty laugh.

"Me, too. And I hope it doesn't take Gram too long to find a new cat."

"That shouldn't be a problem."

"It wouldn't be if Gram didn't have her heart set on a male kitten who looks as much like Hercules as possible. He was totally black, except for a tiny speck of white on his chest." She paused, adding, "Well, how was *your* day? Anything new on the subway killer?"

"We've located one of the few people who witnessed a fainting and assisted a victim but didn't give their names at the scene. The word's out on radio and TV and in the newspapers that we need any information they might have. And we've interviewed the husband of one of the victims, and the men in the lives of the other two," he replied.

"So, only one of the victims was married?"

He consulted his notebook. "Yeah. Justine Meister. She was a receptionist for a Wall Street firm. Her husband owns a pest-control business."

"According to Dan, traces of cyanide showed up in the autopsies," Liz said. "Cyanide is used for pest control, isn't it?"

"Yeah, but the lethal mixture included other toxic substances. It's as if the killer wanted to make sure the mixture was deadly."

"Did all three mixtures contain the same amount of each poison?"

He shook his head. "No. The measurements varied."

"That sounds as if the killer wasn't accustomed to mixing lethal doses," Liz said. "Seems to me the pest-control husband wouldn't be so haphazard. He'd know exactly what to use and how much."

Ike cast her an approving glance. "Good observation. Our thoughts, exactly."

He consulted his notebook again. "The second victim, Valerie Dawes, was a nurse in the office of a medical

practice—two dermatologists. According to other office personnel, she'd been dating one of the physicians
for several months—Dr. Alvin Feldman. In the interview, he seemed genuinely stunned—all broken up."

"A doctor!" Liz's mind teemed with images of hypodermic needles.

"Yeah, but the doorman has him in the office building at nine A.M., and the medics had Valerie in the ambulance at eight fifty-seven. Another thing: A doctor
wouldn't have to rely on a mishmash of poisons—he'd
know what would work."

"Unless he used the mishmash to divert suspicion
from himself," Liz said.

Ike shot her another approving glance. "We haven't
ruled that out. We'll pick up more in our next round of
interviews at the doctors' office. We didn't interview
the other physician yet—Dr. Herman Feldman. He was
out of the office."

"Another Feldman? Are they brothers?"

"No, father and son. Apparently the old man's getting ready to retire."

Dr. Herman Feldman. The name reminded Liz of an
old NYPD colleague of Pop's—Detective Herman
Rivkin. She'd been about eleven when he'd retired
from the force, but she remembered him as a nice old
man who always kept lollipops for her in his desk when
Pop brought her to visit the squad room. She also remembered overhearing talk between her parents and
learning that Detective Rivkin was an Orthodox Jew
who adhered strictly to the tenets of his faith.

But a remark she overheard Pop make to Mom had

intrigued her and left an indelible impression on her young mind. *"If one of Rivkin's kids married a Gentile, he or she would be considered dead."*

Now, that long-ago remark stirred her imagination. *What if the elder Dr. Feldman was a strict Orthodox Jew, and his office nurse, Valerie Dawes, was a Gentile? What if his son told him he intended to marry Valerie? To avoid having to follow the dictates of his faith and declare his son dead, might the elder Feldman have taken drastic action to make sure the marriage did not occur?*

She expressed these thoughts to Ike, adding, "It seems too bizarre, but do you suppose he'd kill to keep his son alive to him?"

"In murder cases, nothing is ever too bizarre," Ike replied. "It's an interesting idea. I'll hang on to it."

Liz felt sure he was thinking, just as she was, of the question surrounding the idea. If the doctor's religious beliefs had led him to eliminate the Gentile woman from his son's life, why would he also kill two other women?

With a shake of her head, Liz turned her thoughts to the third victim. "What did you find out about number three?" she asked.

Ike looked through his notes. "Name's Chloe LaFleur," he replied. "She was a photographer's model. Before we knew it was a homicide, the uniforms checked her apartment to find out how to contact her family, and it turns out her real name is Clara Loffler."

"I guess she thought Chloe LaFleur sounded more glamorous for a model," Liz said. "Did she have a steady boyfriend for you to interview?"

"Make that multiple." Ike flipped the pages of his notebook and read off some names. "Marco Denali . . . Eddie Gund . . . Giles Sinclair."

"Did you interview all of them?"

"Yeah. So far their alibis check out. And get this— from what we picked up, each guy thought he was Chloe's one and only."

"Maybe one of them found out he wasn't," Liz said. "Jealousy can be a powerful motive."

"We're working on that angle," Ike replied. "But there's another man in Chloe's life—a cameraman, Bernie Weiss. Witnesses at his studio told us the two of them had a heated argument just before she left the studio the evening she was killed."

Liz gave this some thought. "Wouldn't it be cutting the time element pretty close for the cameraman to have done it?" she asked. "He would have had to tail her to the subway."

"Yeah, but witnesses to the argument were vague about exactly when he left the studio after Chloe took off. Nobody remembered exactly when he left. In our next round of interviews at the studio, we hope to pin down what the argument was about and the exact time when each of them left there."

"So you have four suspects surrounding Chloe the model. One's a cameraman. What do the other three do for a living?"

Again, Ike looked at his notes. "Denali owns and operates a fleet of limos, Gund is in the wholesale baking business, and Sinclair's in investment banking."

Three boyfriends and a cameraman, Liz thought, and

nothing about any of their professions to suggest poisonous hypos. "How did they react during the interviews?" she asked.

"They all appeared shocked, of course. At the time of the individual interviews, the three boyfriends weren't aware, yet, that Chloe was stringing them all along. That'll leak out on the news by morning."

"Did you notice if one of the three boyfriends seemed more shocked than the others?" she asked. If one were guilty, he could have been putting on an act, she thought.

"Denali seemed the most emotional. Gund and Sinclair seemed fairly calm."

"How about the cameraman?"

"Weiss appeared more angry than anything else. Lou and I agreed he seemed to have a chip on his shoulder."

"Maybe because of the argument he and Chloe had the night she died," Liz said. "Maybe he realizes he could be a suspect. But what would his motive have been? Sure, they had a fight, but . . ."

"This might not have been their first run-in," Ike replied. "Maybe they'd been feuding for a long time, and this last argument pushed him over the edge." He shook his head. "No matter what motives any of the possible suspects might have had for killing a wife or girlfriend, it still doesn't explain why he'd kill the two other women. As far as we know, none of the men we interviewed knew all three victims. He smiled. "Maybe Sophie's idea about a red-haired woman making the killer's life miserable isn't so far out."

"This is only day one of your investigation," Liz

said. "There's no telling what new information you'll dig up tomorrow."

He nodded. "We'll need all the new information we can get. This is going to be a tough one."

Ike's words resounded in her mind long after he left and she'd settled into her sofa bed. This was, indeed, going to be a tough case. Too many murders. Too many possible suspects. Too many weak motives.

And no common denominator except the victims' red hair.

Chapter Five

By the next morning, when Liz turned off her alarm clock and switched on her TV, the subway murders had taken over the news media. It was as if the seeds of information in the initial reporting had germinated overnight like rampant weeds. Yesterday, the victims had only been identified by name. Today, their photos were on every news channel, along with statements from family members down to casual acquaintances. Liz had no doubt that photos would be plastered all over the daily newspapers, with in-depth information concerning the victims.

The weather report predicted another unseasonably warm day, with no change. That meant work-bound women would again be wearing light clothing. Well, at least those with red hair now knew that a ride on the Lex local could be their last unless they covered their heads. *Or dyed their hair.*

45

While brewing her coffee, she listened to a perky female commentator report on the love life of beautiful photographer's model, victim Chloe LaFleur. Ike was right. Word that she was seeing three men had leaked out, along with their names. Reporters had done plenty of nosing around last night, she thought. She figured all three of Chloe's swains must know, by now, that she'd been two-timing them—or, in this case, *three*-timing.

"Stand by for additional coverage of the subway homicides, after these messages," the newscaster said.

Maybe there'd be some live footage of the men who'd been interviewed by the police, Liz thought. She reviewed them all in her mind, starting with Chloe's three boyfriends—the limo fleet proprietor, the chain bakery owner, and the investment banker, plus the cameraman. This big lineup almost overshadowed the pest-control husband and the father-and-son doctors.

News reporters and photographers might not get interviews or shots of the possible suspects today, she thought, especially Marco Denali, the younger Dr. Feldman, and Otto Meister. Wouldn't those bereaved men skip work for a day after the death of a fiancée or wife and be inaccessible to the media?

By the time she thawed a bagel in the microwave and refilled her coffee mug, the news was back on. To her surprise, live shots were shown of Otto Meister, the pest-control husband emerging from his apartment building, dressed in coveralls with a logo, OTTO'S EXTERMINATING CO. It looked as if he were on his way to work. A crowd of waiting reporters and photographers immediately surged around him, firing questions.

She remembered Ike's saying that Otto Meister had been uncooperative during his initial interview; thus, she wasn't surprised when he refused to speak to the reporters other than to call them unflattering names. He also gave one of them a hefty push and tried to grab a camera away from another.

Well, reporters shouldn't be badgering the poor guy so soon after his wife's murder, she thought. No wonder he was so belligerent. As an afterthought she asked herself if business as usual wasn't somewhat strange for a husband so recently bereaved.

Abruptly, coverage switched to reporters gathered outside a building. When Liz saw a sign over the entrance saying DENALI'S DELUXE TRANSPORTATION and noticed a man making his way through the crowd, her senses went on alert. Was he Marco Denali? According to Ike, of all the men in victim Chloe's life, the limo fleet operator had shown the most emotion during his interview. She felt surprised that he, too, would not remain in seclusion today.

Moments later, cameras zoomed in on the man's face. Liz caught her breath. If he were Marco Denali, why did Chloe even so much as glance at another man? *This guy was a Dean Martin look-alike!* Although she and Sophie were barely into their teens when the legendary singer, entertainer, and film star died, they'd discovered him via old movies and recordings. For a while, he was their idol. While their friends swooned over various contemporary stars of Hollywood and the music world, for Sophie and Liz, none of them even came close to Dean in sheer masculine appeal and the ability to belt out songs.

Reporters surged around the look-alike. Hearing them call out his name, Liz knew he was Marco Denali. Studying his handsome face, his crest of dark hair, and his dark eyes, she could almost hear Dean singing "That's Amore."

Unlike Otto Meister, he was cooperative. "I'll answer questions as best I can," he told the reporters. "But you must understand, my fiancée's death was a terrible shock, and—"

A reporter's voice broke in, loud and clear, above the hubbub. "Are you saying you and Chloe LaFleur were planning to marry?"

Marco nodded. "That's what I'm saying."

Liz braced herself for the reporters' inevitable questions concerning Chloe's multiple romances.

"If you were planning a marriage, how come she was seeing two other men?"

"And why wasn't she wearing an engagement ring?"

Marco's handsome faced clouded, but he answered both questions calmly and convincingly. "A woman as beautiful as my fiancée would naturally have many admirers. After we got engaged, we agreed she should let the others down easy—let them know, gradually, that she wouldn't be seeing them anymore. As for the engagement ring, I'd selected a diamond. It was being set." He paused. His voice faltered as he added, "I was going to give it to her tonight."

With that, he brushed at his eyes, bowed his head, and turned away, saying, "I'm sure you'll excuse me for not answering any more questions."

Watching him go into the building, Liz wondered if

this emotional scene was on the level or whether it was a performance worthy of Dean Martin himself.

The newscaster came on, promising more subway homicide news after a few commercials. Liz checked the time and knew she should get going. Maybe she could catch the rest of this on her office TV, she thought. If not, she wouldn't miss anything. There'd be reruns throughout the day.

At a newsstand near the subway station, Liz noticed that both the *Post* and *Daily News* featured front-page photos of the three victims. Like the photos shown on TV, the pictures of Chloe were glamour shots. In the *Post*, she was wearing a bikini; in the *News*, she was wrapped in white fur. In both newspapers, photos of Justine and Valerie looked as if they'd been taken from high school yearbooks. Reporters would have had no trouble getting their hands on shots of a successful New York model, Liz thought. They'd probably had to scrounge for the pictures of the other two.

Looking at the three faces, she felt a renewal of her initial shock and horror. Three young women, whose hair color had made them victims of a crazed killer.

She bought a copy of the *Post*. It was a relief to know she wouldn't have to try to head off another subway homicide this morning. After all the publicity, any redheads aboard would be well disguised. Also, she suspected there'd be plainclothes cops in the cars. Locking the barn after the horse was gone? Maybe not. It would take only one wisp of hair straying from beneath a scarf to get the killer seeing red again.

On the train, she read the rest of the newspaper—
mostly articles on the victims' backgrounds. Investiga-
tive reporters had obtained plenty of information about
all three.

Chloe's small-town roots, her success as a New York
model, and her three-way love life were described in de-
tail. Reading what relatives and townspeople had to say,
Liz found out that Chloe was estranged from her family.

"She hated Bronson's Corners—called it a hick town,"
a woman who'd grown up with Chloe told a reporter.

"Everybody knew she wanted to leave," a former
teacher stated.

"She took off as soon as she saved enough money
working in her father's grain and feed store," an uncle
said.

Liz was surprised that the parents of the other two
victims had been interviewed, and their statements, with
some rather intimate details, included in the articles.
If *she'd* been murdered, would Pop and Mom want to
be interviewed by the news media so soon afterward?
Maybe, in their shock, such bereaved parents felt the
need to talk about it.

Valerie's plain, middle-class upbringing in Brooklyn,
her job in a medical practice as a so-called nurse, and her
romance with one of the physicians were fully covered.
Quotes by her parents, both apparently respectable, hard-
working people, made Liz feel they'd been pleased with
the prospect of Valerie's marrying Dr. Alvin Feldman.

"We were never able to give her the kind of life she
wanted," her father told reporters.

"Being the wife of a wealthy doctor would have made her happy," her mother stated.

Justine's affluent family life in an upscale New York suburb, her position as receptionist in a prestigious Wall Street firm, and her parents' disapproval of her marriage were reported in depth. Remorseful statements by Justine's mother and father made Liz conclude they'd disowned her for marrying against their wishes.

"If we had it to do all over again, we wouldn't have been so harsh."

"We thought if we cut her off, she'd come to her senses."

Why had they disapproved of Otto? Liz wondered. Did they think a blue-collar working husband was not worthy of their daughter, or was there some other reason they disliked him?

Soon after Liz arrived at work, Sophie phoned from the squad car, saying that she and her partner, Mike, were on their way to a robbery scene. "I gotta make this quick," she said. "But I couldn't wait to tell you some good news. Ralph's been okayed for detective training."

"Oh, Sophie, that's great!"

"Yeah, he just found out and called me a few minutes ago. Can you and Ike come to our place for dinner tonight and celebrate with us?"

"I'm pretty sure we can. I'll run it by Ike."

"We're at the scene," Sophie said. "I'll call you later."

Liz smiled as she hung up the phone. Ike would be as pleased as she about this. They both knew Ralph had his heart set on it. He'd applied for detective training as soon as he was eligible. His goal was to be in Homicide.

At that moment, she saw Dan approaching her desk with his usual smile. If another red-haired woman had been brought to the morgue that morning, he'd be looking grim, she thought.

"I just stopped by on my way to the elevator to say good morning and have another look at that hair of yours," he said. "If I hadn't known you since you were a carrottopped kid, I'd swear you're a real brunet."

"Good morning, Dan. All quiet on the subway?"

He nodded. "With every redhead in the city avoiding the six train, or hiding her hair or dying it or wearing a wig, our killer's fresh out of targets." With another smile, he went on his way.

Watching him go, Liz asked herself if this could really be the last of it. What if the killer decided that every woman whose hair was hidden by a scarf or a hat had to be a redhead? Or what if an obvious blond or brunet wig made him believe there was red hair under there? Or suppose someone had a poor dye job? She breathed a thankful sigh that hers had turned out looking natural.

As long as the weather stayed warm, women would continue to wear clothing light enough for the killer to jab a needle through, she thought. Until he was caught, there was no certainty that he would not target another victim. Dan was aware of this, she decided. His remarks were meant to reassure her.

During the afternoon she found time to turn on her desk TV and catch up with the news. A live interview with Chloe's cameraman, Bernie Weiss, had just started. He was a short, dark-haired young man with shaggy eyebrows and eyes too squinty to determine their color. Maybe they'd gotten that way from constantly squinting into his camera, she thought, but whatever the cause, it made him appear both unattractive and untrustworthy. She told herself that was unfair, but the impression stayed with her during the interview.

"I gave Chloe her first break," Bernie Weiss said. "And who do you think gave her the idea of changing her name?" He paused with a semi sneer. "While she was Clara Loffler, she was just part of the pack of pretty models trying to make it in New York."

This guy sounded bitter, Liz thought. Had he fallen for Clara Loffler and found himself brushed off by Chloe LaFleur?

A voice rose from the cluster of reporters. "If she was just one of the pack, how come the two of you started working together so closely?"

"I'd worked with enough models to recognize she had great possibilities," Bernie replied. "I asked for her every chance I got. I taught her how to move with the camera. I made sure I always got her best angles. And I was the one who came up with the glamorous name. When I recommended her to the ad agency that represented a top cosmetics company, that's when her career took off."

He paused, his shaggy brows clashing above his squinty eyes. "It didn't take long for her to get too big for her britches."

Liz stared at the screen. Chloe had been murdered

only two days ago. Bad-mouthing her on national TV was the mark of a first-class jerk.

Perhaps the news programmer agreed. Coverage of Bernie Weiss ended. "Stand by for a taped interview with bakery magnate Edgar Gund, another man in the life of Chloe LaFleur," the newscaster said.

A camera zoomed in on a corpulent, middle-aged man alighting from a chauffeur-driven Lincoln Town Car in front of a large building. Eddie Gund looked as if he'd eaten too many of his well-advertised Granny Gund's Goodies, Liz thought.

A startled expression appeared on his round face when reporters started firing a barrage of questions at him. Liz recoiled at their insensitivity.

How long had he known Chloe LaFleur? What was their relationship? Was he surprised when he found out she was seeing other men? Did he know she was engaged to marry one of them? Did he have any idea who'd want to kill her?

Gund impressed Liz as mild-mannered. "It's difficult to answer so many individual questions," he told the reporters. "Instead, I'll make a general statement. I have known Miss LaFleur since she was featured in our advertising a few months ago. Our relationship was strictly friendship. I was shocked and saddened when I learned what happened to her. She was a sweet little lady, and I can't imagine why anyone would want to kill her." Ignoring further shouted questions, he held up a pudgy hand to indicate he'd said all he was going to, and hurried into his building. He certainly didn't come across as a bereaved lover, Liz thought.

The coverage ended. The newscaster returned to the screen, saying, "Stay tuned for further news after these messages."

No media interviews, yet, with the father-and-son doctors or with investment banker Giles Sinclair, she thought, turning off the set. But Ike must have talked with them by now.

Ike phoned a few moments later. She told him the news about Ralph's making it into detective training. Ralph was not in the same precinct as Ike; thus, Ike hadn't heard.

"Great news," he said. "Ralph has the makings of a first-rate detective."

"Sophie invited us over for a celebration dinner tonight," Liz told him.

"Good," he replied. "I could do with a little celebrating. This case is getting more complicated every day."

"Did you interview the two doctors and the banker today?" she asked.

"Yeah, we did our first interview with the elder doc and a follow-up with the son, and then the banker. I'll give you a rundown when I see you tonight."

Something in his voice when he mentioned the elder doctor made her think that Dr. Herman Feldman hadn't been cooperative. But, as always, Ike wouldn't go into it on the phone. She'd have to wait until tonight to find out if he believed that strong religious doctrines could have possibly led to murder.

Chapter Six

"Here's to Ralph's detective career," Ike said, raising his wineglass.

"Investigating homicides," Sophie added.

They were in the kitchen of Sophie and Ralph's apartment. Sophie was making pirogis, chicken breasts were turning crusty brown under the broiler, and Ralph was putting a salad together.

Liz held back an envious sigh. Unlike her tiny makeshift kitchenette where two people could barely fit, here all four of them could hang out without bumping elbows. Besides plenty of cabinets and counter space, there was room in front of the window for a round table and four chairs. But a moment later the inward sigh gave way to a smile. It wouldn't be long before she and Ike would have their own large kitchen.

"Your table looks elegant," she said, looking at the white cloth and napkins, candles in silver holders, gleaming flatware, ivory-colored, gold-rimmed china plates, and the small arrangement of miniature yellow roses she and Ike had picked up at the market on their way over.

Sophie nodded. "It does look nice, doesn't it? With the flowers you brought, it could be on the cover of *House Beautiful.*"

"We don't usually eat this fancy, but tonight Sophie wanted us to use our wedding china and a bunch of other wedding presents," Ralph said.

"Why not?" Liz asked. "This is a special occasion."

"Yeah," Ike said, slapping Ralph on the back. "You're going to make one hell of a homicide detective."

"Thanks. Let's hope it turns out that way," Ralph replied.

"Sure it will," Ike said. "Maybe you can get in some practice tonight when we start swapping ideas about the subway homicides. I guess we all saw the TV interviews with the possible suspects—all except the two doctors and the banker. The media haven't caught up with those three yet, but I'll tell you how our own interviews went."

Sophie's voice came into the talk. "The pirogis are ready, and so's the chicken. You guys sit down, and Liz and I will bring the plates. We can discuss the case while we eat."

For the next few moments, Liz wondered when they'd get around to talking about the subway homicides. After Ike bit into his first pirogi, he seemed to have forgotten his promise to tell them about his interviews with Giles Sinclair and the father-and-son dermatologists.

"Great chow, Sophie," he said. "I've never eaten this before. Is it traditional Polish food?"

"Yes. This is one of my grandmother Bencoweicz's recipes from the Old Country."

Ralph gave a chuckle. "Speaking of ethnic food—my mother was worried when I told her I was going to marry a girl named Pulaski. 'She won't know how to cook Italian,' Ma said. Like I'd starve to death."

"With Rosa Moscaretti just downstairs, Ike and I will never have to learn how to cook Italian," Liz said.

Ike nodded. "But Liz's grandmother showed her how to make a supergood Irish stew, and I'm up on all the best take-out places."

"Now that everyone knows we're in no danger of starving, how about a rundown on your interviews with the banker and the dermatologists?" Liz asked.

Ike popped another pirogi into his mouth and savored it, before replying, "Sure. Here goes."

She was especially curious about the elder Dr. Feldman, but Ike began with Giles Sinclair. He and Lou had interviewed the investment banker in his office.

"He was fully cooperative. He seemed more concerned about embarrassing his high-society family than anything else. He told us the Sinclairs have lived in Manhattan since Theodore Roosevelt was New York's police commissioner."

"Did he seem surprised about Chloe's other boyfriends?" Liz asked. *Especially about Marco Denali's reference to her as his fiancée?*

"Surprised, yes, but unemotional. We got the feeling he wasn't serious about Chloe."

"Just having a little fling before settling down with some family-approved babe?" Ralph asked.

"Right," Ike replied. "We figured if he had found out about Chloe's other boyfriends, he wouldn't have been jealous and angry enough to kill. We're close to striking Sinclair off our list."

Liz did a quick mental review of the other men in Chloe LaFleur's life. On TV, Eddie Gund had come across as too mild a man to commit murder. Besides, he looked more like an uncle than a lover, and he'd insisted they were just friends.

On the other hand, Marco Denali had claimed he and Chloe were engaged and said he knew about the other men. But suppose this was a lie? Despite his Dean Martin looks, on TV, Marco impressed her as a man who might have an explosive temper.

And she mustn't overlook cameraman Bernie Weiss. He'd bad-mouthed Chloe on TV. Obviously, he disliked her. Enough to want her dead?

"So you're ready to strike Sinclair. How do things stand with the other possible suspects in Chloe's murder?" she asked.

Ike consulted his notebook. "Starting with Gund— he's definitely in there. His phone records show a high number of calls to Chloe during the past six weeks, and a search of her apartment turned up two letters he'd written to her."

"Love letters?" Liz and Sophie chorused.

"Yeah. No doubt about it. He lied about their being just friends. That angle should break on the news any time now."

"With the contents of the letters spelled out?" Liz asked.

Ike laughed. "No. We only released a statement saying letters were found that suggest that Gund might have had more than a friendly interest in Chloe."

Sophie rose and turned on a small TV on top of the refrigerator. "You can bet there'll be plenty of media speculation about this. I'll keep the volume on mute while Ike fills us in, but I want to catch the love letters report as soon as it breaks."

"Me, too," Liz replied. She pictured the mild-mannered Eddie Gund being besieged by reporters again. How would he react to being caught in a lie?

"Meanwhile, I'll fill you in on the two doctors," Ike said. "With the younger doc, it was a follow-up. Nothing new. He was just as broken up about his girlfriend's murder as he was the first time around. I've seen enough faked grief to recognize the real thing. That, and his airtight alibi has us ready to strike him off the list."

Liz waited for him to get around to the elder physician. She still wondered if his religion could possibly have led him to eliminate his son's Gentile girlfriend rather than proclaim his son dead.

Just as Ike was about to go on with his report, Sophie gave a squeal and pointed to the TV. "Look! There's Dr. Herman Feldman. I recognize him from the newspaper photo."

She turned up the sound. They heard reporters shouting questions at the doctor as he emerged from his office building. Liz judged he was in his late sixties. His dark eyes glared from behind glasses halfway down on his prominent nose. He looked very angry.

"I said everything to the police already," he stated, making his way toward a waiting vehicle—a BMW, Liz noticed. A driver, springing to open the rear door, looked as if he regularly lifted weights.

"Did you approve of your son's relationship with Valerie Dawes?" a female reporter called out.

Scowling, Dr. Feldman ignored the question.

When the driver moved to assist him through the crowd, Liz thought this might develop into a repeat of the Otto Meister vs. reporters scene. But, whether in deference to the doctor's age or the driver's muscles, the reporters backed off. Moments later, Dr. Feldman was inside the car being driven off.

Watching, Liz remembered the doctor's angry eyes. Again, she asked herself if that anger could have been a vestige of religious fanaticism flaring out of control.

"Looks like the reporters didn't get anywhere with the old doc," Ralph said. "Ike, let's hear about your interview with him."

"After what you just saw, I'm sure you all got a pretty good idea how it went," Ike replied. "He's an uncooperative grouch. We had to drag answers out of him. But while we were there, we picked up something interesting. Valerie wasn't the only attractive young nurse working for the two doctors. There's another one. Name's Amy Baron. When we questioned her, we got the strong feeling she wasn't shedding any tears over Valerie."

Liz's imagination was activated. *Did this Amy Baron want young Dr. Alvin Feldman for herself? Jealousy could lead to murder.*

Evidently Ralph had the same idea. "Any chance this other nurse had something to do with killing Valerie?" he asked.

"No," Ike replied. "At the time Valerie collapsed in the subway, Nurse Amy was in the office. The young doc corroborated this."

"Maybe Amy and the younger doctor were in cahoots," Ralph suggested.

Ike shook his head. "The young doc was genuinely broken up about Valerie. If he can fake that kind of emotion, he should win an Oscar."

Liz mulled this over. Apparently the younger Feldman didn't figure into a plot to do away with Valerie, but if Amy Baron were Jewish, the elder doctor might approve of her as a wife for his son. Suppose the two of them conspired to get rid of the *shiksa*.

When she ran the idea past Ike, he told her he'd considered that possibility.

"I should have known you'd pick up on that," she said.

"That's what I get paid for," he replied. "But since Amy was nowhere near the subway when Valerie collapsed, we ruled it out."

"Did the old doc have an alibi for that morning?" Ralph asked.

Liz remembered Ike's saying the elder Feldman was out of the office when he interviewed the son for the first time. "Good question," she said. "Where was he when Valerie passed out?"

"He was attending a medical conference in Atlantic City," Ike replied. "He didn't get back until today. That's why we didn't interview him sooner."

Liz thought this through. Ike would have made certain that Dr. Herman Feldman had actually attended the medical conference. He would have verified the date and time when the doctor signed in at the conference. But Atlantic City wasn't too long a drive from Manhattan. Suppose he'd been driven there in his BMW, signed in, come back to Manhattan to get rid of Valerie, then returned to Atlantic City.

After further thought, the notion seemed terribly far-fetched: elderly Dr. Feldman lurking in the subway crush, poisoned hypodermic needle in hand, waiting for Valerie to appear. Besides, his driver would have been questioned.

Still, she couldn't shake the idea that Dr. Herman Feldman and the possibly Jewish nurse who wanted his son had teamed up to eliminate Valerie.

Up until now, she'd been going along with the concept of a lone male stalking and killing young, red-haired women on the subway. The emergence of Amy Baron widened the focus. Far-fetched as it seemed, especially when she asked herself why the other redheads were murdered, she wasn't ready to rule out a conspiracy in the murder of Valerie Dawes.

If she could meet Amy Baron and the elder doctor face-to-face, she might be able to detect something between them and perhaps determine if they were capable of such a conspiracy.

The idea lingered in the back of her mind for the rest of the evening.

Chapter Seven

What a great time they'd had last night, Liz thought when she awakened the next morning. Enjoying Sophie's Polish meal and tossing around a lot of ideas about the subway murders had made it a fun evening.

Ike had lingered awhile after he brought her home. She didn't tell him about wanting to meet the elder Feldman and Nurse Amy face-to-face. Even when she decided how she was going to do this, she'd still keep it to herself. She didn't want her kindling plan to be doused by his disapproval. Instead of discussing the subway murders, they'd snuggled on the sofa and talked about their forthcoming wedding and living in the spacious apartment soon to be vacated by the Moscarettis' other tenant.

Now, she turned on the TV to the Weather Channel. The day's forecast predicted one more day of unseasonably mild temperatures. Another day when women would be wearing light clothing. Another day for red-headed women to keep their hair out of sight.

In the bathroom, she gazed into the mirror at her brown hair, thankful that she was no longer a target, hoping that the women who *were* would continue being careful.

The killer had struck three times between Monday and Tuesday evenings. Now it was Friday, but just because there'd been no more subway homicides in the last couple of days didn't mean it was over. Maybe the killer was waiting for his red-haired targets to relax and get careless, or maybe, for some reason, he was waiting for his earlier victims' funerals to be over. According to the news media, Chloe's body had been taken to her hometown in Kansas. The funeral was to be held tomorrow. Services for Justine were to take place in a suburban New York church today. Plans for Valerie's funeral had been put on hold until her brother, serving with the military in the Middle East, could get leave to attend.

Even after last evening's speculation, she was still thinking of the killer as a lone male. But now she thought about Amy Baron again and wished there were some way she could meet her, face-to-face. Maybe then she'd be able to judge whether or not Nurse Amy could possibly be capable of plotting murder with the elder doctor.

On her way to work, she phoned Gram to get an update on the quest for a new cat.

"No luck so far," Gram reported. "Mrs. Dugan over on Locust Street—her cat had a litter a month or so ago, and she told me there were two black kittens, but when I went to see them, one had white paws and a white face, and the other was all black but a female."

"Couldn't you settle for an all-black female?" Liz asked.

She could picture Gram shaking her head. "Her face didn't have the right look."

Liz remembered that look. Even as a kitten, Hercules had had a jowly face. "Well, don't get discouraged," she said. "You'll find the right one sooner or later."

Ike phoned her at work during the afternoon. The instant she heard his voice, she sensed something was bothering him. "Are you okay?" she asked.

"Physically okay," he replied. "Mentally, not so hot."

"What's wrong?"

"Lou and I won't be handling the subway homicides alone anymore. The lieutenant just told us that the commissioner wants more detectives on the case."

"That's understandable," she replied, hoping to make him realize this was no reflection on the Eichle and Sanchez duo. "With three victims and so many possible suspects, you could use some help."

"Yeah, that's how the lieutenant explained it," Ike replied.

"Who's coming in on it?" she asked.

"We don't know yet." His voice sounded glum.

"Cheer up," she said. "This way you won't have to put in too much overtime."

"We're going to put in plenty, anyway." Suddenly his voice brightened. "I almost forgot—I might have some good news for you about finding a cat for Gram."

Where would he have stumbled upon a possible replacement for Hercules? she wondered. Before she could ask, he started to explain.

"Several physicians and veterinarians have reported thefts of drugs within the past week," he said. "Lou and I thought there might be a tie-in with the subway murders, so we dropped in at their various offices this morning."

For a moment, Liz couldn't decide if she were more interested in a possible replacement for Hercules or a possible link to the subway murders. The murders took priority. "What did you find out?" she asked.

"Nothing for you to latch on to," he replied. "The initial police reports indicated break-ins. All these doctors' offices were on the ground floor, and there was evidence of lock-picking and window jimmying, and in one veterinarian's office a windowpane had been smashed in the room where the drugs were stored. The cops had already suggested that they add extra locks or install alarm systems. We advised Dr. Jurgens, the vet with the smashed window, to move the drugs to a room with no outside access, and we're contacting all Manhattan veterinarians to take similar precautions."

"So, what about Gram's cat?" Liz asked.

"I was getting to that," Ike replied. "While we were at Dr. Jurgens', I noticed a crate of kittens for adoption. One was black, and a staff member told me it's a male. I told Dr. Jurgens about your grandmother's looking for a black male kitten to replace Hercules and gave her your name. She said she'd hold the kitten for you until you could get in to see him. Her office isn't too far from yours. Maybe you could go there after work and have a look. You want the address?"

"Oh, yes! You're sure the black kitten doesn't have any white on him?"

"Just a small stripe on his chest."

"Oh, Ike, that's exactly what Gram wants!"

"Okay, here's the address. . . ."

"Thanks," she said, taking it down. "And thanks for remembering Gram was looking for a new cat, and for being so thoughtful."

"Glad to be of help," he replied. "I'll see you tonight. I might be a little late."

His voice sounded downcast again. Sharing an investigation was a blow to his pride, she thought as she clicked off the phone. It had never happened to him before. But he'd never worked on a case like this before, either. There hadn't been a serial killer in Manhattan since Ike made detective.

She remembered Pop's talking about the Son of Sam serial murders, a case that had gripped New York in fear for months, more than thirty years ago. Pop hadn't said how many detectives were assigned to that one, but she was willing to bet every squad in the city was in on it.

She sensed that Ike wanted to be the detective who cracked this case. If only she could come up with something to help him, as she had with other homicides, when her amateur sleuthing had turned up information that led to vital clues. She smiled, remembering what Ike had once said to her. *"It's getting so I can't solve a case without you."* She knew he was joking. He'd have wrapped up every one. What he was telling her was, without her input, it might have taken much longer.

She wanted Ike to get credit for nabbing the subway killer. Although the case was more complicated than any she'd ever delved into, she decided to make every effort. Maybe she'd be lucky enough to stumble on to something this time, too.

Ike said he'd be late tonight. She'd have plenty of time to check on the kitten at the vet's, and then shop for groceries.

Although darkness had fallen when she left her office, there was nothing else to indicate that it was December. The temperature still felt as mild as May. But it wouldn't last, she thought, remembering this morning's weather forecast. By tomorrow it would be cold, and women riding the subway would be wearing heavy jackets or coats. Tonight might be the subway killer's last chance to easily needle another red-haired victim.

Her thoughts turned to Gram's prospective kitten. Although Dr. Jurgens' office was several long blocks away, she decided to walk the distance. From Ike's description, she felt almost positive the search for another Hercules was over, but she wanted to wait until she'd seen the kitten before phoning Gram.

Dr. Jurgens' waiting room was divided into two sections—cats on one side, dogs on the other. Liz noticed that both sections were empty, most likely because it was near closing time. A receptionist seated at a counter between the two sections smiled at her, asking if she'd come to pick up a pet.

At that moment, Liz saw a crate alongside the counter, with a sign on it: KITTENS FOR ADOPTION.

"No, but I'm interested in adopting a kitten," she replied.

She peered into the crate. Her heart bounded when she located the lone black kitten in the litter.

The receptionist must have noticed her excitement. She smiled again, saying, "If you see one you like, I'll bring it out."

Liz nodded. "Yes, thanks—I'd like to see the black one."

Moments later she was holding the dark, furry body in her arms, knowing without the slightest doubt that he was Hercules Junior. "I'd like to adopt this one," she said.

Just then, the door on the dogs' side of the waiting room opened, and an elderly man came out with a golden retriever on a leash. A tall, sturdy-looking woman wearing a white lab coat accompanied him. She had slightly graying brown hair and looked to be in her midfifties. Liz guessed she was Dr. Jurgens.

"He'll be fine, now, Mr. Pratt," Liz heard her say. "Make sure he doesn't get into any more chicken bones."

She turned to the receptionist, saying, "Well, Gail, that does it for today." Then she saw Liz holding the kitten.

"Are you Liz Rooney, the detective's friend?" she asked.

"Yes," Liz replied, cuddling the small, furry body.

The veterinarian smiled. "Have we found a home for little Blackie?"

"Oh, yes!" Liz exclaimed. "He's exactly what my grandmother wants."

Dr. Jurgens smiled. "Great. I can tell you want to take him home as soon as possible, but he needs to be neutered and given his shots." She paused, looking regretful. "I wish I could get to him tomorrow, but . . ." Her voice trailed off, as if she were picturing multiple treatments and surgeries. "I'm afraid you'll have to wait till Monday or Tuesday," she said.

"Doctor, I was just going to tell you, we got a postponement a few minutes ago on tomorrow's ten A.M. spay job," the receptionist said.

Dr. Jurgens turned to Liz with a big smile. "Good. We can schedule your kitten for that time slot." Smiling, she held out her arms. "I'll take him to his overnight quarters."

"Thanks," Liz said. She gave the kitten a farewell pat and handed him over.

"Leave your name and phone number with Gail, and she'll phone you tomorrow when he's ready to be picked up," Dr. Jurgens said, as she left the waiting room.

The clock above the receptionist's counter showed only a few seconds remaining till six. Liz noticed the receptionist starting to clear her workstation.

"Good night, Gail. I'll be waiting for your call tomorrow," she said.

"Good night," the receptionist replied, switching off the light above the counter.

Out of the corner of her eye, Liz saw the veterinarian's assistants, two young women and a young man, coming out the door through which Dr. Jurgens had gone. They walked to the entrance, calling good night to the receptionist. Liz turned to follow them out the door, when suddenly a closer look at the young woman just ahead of her made her catch her breath. The woman's hair, falling long and loose well below her shoulders, was the color of burnished copper!

Chapter Eight

For the past hour or so, she hadn't thought about the subway homicides. Gram and the kitten had taken over her mind. Now, the cascade of red hair on the young woman leaving the office just ahead of her brought it all back.

If this woman were taking a subway home, she'd probably be headed for the very one on which the three redheads had been murdered. It was only a short walk away. Didn't she realize the danger? That head of hair would stand out in the rush-hour crowd like a bright red banner. Also, she was wearing a sweater so loosely knit that her sleeveless blouse was visible beneath it. She might as well have had a sign on her sleeve saying, *Jab me.*

Liz debated whether or not to say something to her. But surely she knew about the subway killer. Surely she knew that if she got on the six, she'd risk being a target.

Did she think she'd be safe because the killer hadn't struck since Tuesday?

But when the woman walked to the curb and paused, as if she were going to hail a cab, Liz felt a bit foolish. Of course she knew of the danger, and she was taking a taxi instead of the subway.

At that moment, the woman turned and saw Liz staring at her. Liz felt as if she should explain.

"I guess you're looking for a cab," she said, joining her at the curb. "When I noticed your red hair, I was worried. At first I thought you were on your way to the subway."

The woman smiled. "You thought I might not know about the subway killer, and you were going to warm me."

Liz returned the smile. "You'd have to be just in from Mars not to know about it. I thought you might have let your guard down because there've been no more murders since Tuesday."

"Thanks for your concern," the woman said. "If I rode the subway, I'd certainly keep my hair out of sight until the killer's caught. But I detest the subway. I never use it. I take cabs everywhere."

Getting a cab during rush hours wasn't easy, Liz thought. This redhead could be standing at the curb for a long time. "Isn't it inconvenient, waiting for vacant cab after work every night?" she asked.

The woman shook her head. "I never have to wait long. When I first came to Manhattan and started working for Dr. Jurgens, I soon found out how hard it is to get a cab during rush hours, so I made arrangements with a car company to be taken to and from work every day. I have the same driver all the time. It's almost like having my own chauffeur."

She extended her hand. "My name's Paula Rubik. Are you the one who's going to adopt the little black kitten?"

"Yes. I'm Liz Rooney. Actually, I'm getting him for my grandmother."

"Your grandmother will love him, Liz. He's adorable. I see lots of cats, and he's the cutest I've seen in a long time. I'm so glad he's getting a good home."

She peered into the street traffic. "Here comes my car. May I give you a lift somewhere, Liz?"

The car was headed in the opposite direction from where Liz planned to buy her groceries. "Oh, thanks, but I have some shopping to do on my way home, and it would be out of your way," she replied.

"So long then, Liz. I'll see you when you come for the kitten."

"So long . . . Paula."

This Paula Rubik was a nice, friendly person, Liz decided, watching the car drive off. The thought crossed her mind that taxiing everywhere had to be a terrific expense. But that was no concern of hers. She turned her thoughts to Ike and his frame of mind.

Walking to the grocery store, she reviewed her recent phone conversation with him. How downcast he'd sounded when he told her that additional detectives had been assigned to the subway homicide case. Again, she told herself she must do whatever snooping she could to help him. She must come up with something he could grab hold of—something that might lead to a vital clue—something that would make him the one who solved the case.

She'd done it before. She could do it again. She'd start with the Amy Baron angle. How could she determine if Amy were capable of conspiring to murder Valerie Dawes?

In the market, she phoned Gram to tell her she'd found another Hercules.

"Acutally, it was Ike who found him," she said. She gave the details.

Gram sounded ecstatic. "I know you wouldn't be calling me if you weren't absolutely sure he's the right one," she said.

"He's the one, all right. He even has a splash of white on his chest. He's being neutered and given his shots, and we can pick him up at the vet's tomorrow morning."

"I'll come to your place with my cat carrier," Gram replied. "And, when you see Ike tonight, give him a big kiss for me."

She greeted Ike at the door with a double kiss. "One's from Gram," she said.

"Oh, did it work out with the kitten?" he asked.

"It did. Gram's delighted, and so am I. She's coming here tomorrow with her cat carrier, and we're going to pick the kitten up at the vet's."

A slight frown crossed his face. "For a second I thought about Gram's red hair," he said. "But she's savvy enough to wear a hat or something. The train won't be too crowded on a Saturday, and with the weather supposed to turn colder tomorrow, she'll be wearing a heavy coat or jacket. She'll be okay."

Liz nodded. The killer depended on a crush of people to carry out his deadly work. He wouldn't risk jabbing a needle into a woman's arm in an uncrowded car. New Yorkers had the reputation for minding their own business, even in unusual circumstances, but noticing a woman being jabbed would surely spur someone into action.

"Besides, the commissioner's keeping plainclothes cops on the trains over the weekend, just to be on the safe side," Ike said. "And, like I said, the cars won't be overcrowded. Gram might even get a seat."

Liz sensed he was in a lighter mood. "Are you feeling better about sharing the case?" she asked, when they sat down to eat.

He nodded. "I shouldn't have taken it personally. When I thought it over, I realized that this one is too much for Lou and me to handle alone."

"Do you know who's coming in on it?"

"Yeah—Burns and Wolkweicz."

"Those names don't sound familiar. They must have joined the squad after Pop retired."

"Yeah, they've been on a year or so. They're both women."

"Does that bother you?" she asked. Pop had told her that some male squad members hadn't fully accepted working with women. She hoped Ike wasn't one of them.

Her heart warmed when Ike shook his head. "I only hope they're as smart as you, Redlocks."

And she always loved it when he made his joking comparison of her to Sherlock Holmes.

After eating, they took mugs of coffee to the sofa and watched TV news. Random street interviews concerning the subway homicides indicated general dissatisfaction with police progress on the case.

"What do people expect in only three days?" Liz asked indignantly.

"Fear makes people unreasonable," Ike replied.

If she were still a redhead, she'd probably be unreasonable, too, Liz thought. Suddenly, she remembered the woman at Dr. Jurgens'.

"Oh, I wanted to tell you about a woman I met when I went to look at the kitten," she said. "She's one of the doctor's assistants—young, with red hair. Maybe you met her when you and Lou were there."

"Yeah, I recall one of the assistants was a redhead. What about her?"

"She left work at six o'clock with her hair loose and hanging down to her shoulders. I felt I should warn her about the subway killer, so I followed her out of the building." Liz related the conversation.

"I hope she doesn't think taking cabs everywhere means she couldn't be another victim," he replied. "It could happen to a red-haired woman in any crowded place. Serial killers generally stick to one MO, but you can't count on it. That's why dying your hair was a good idea. You're protected, on or off the subway."

"I'm thankful I have a boyfriend clever enough to think of that," she said.

Suddenly, she thought of Dr. Alvin Feldman,

boyfriend of murder victim Valerie. The scenario she'd concocted about his father's disapproval and the possible conspiracy with nurse Amy Baron replayed in her mind. It had been determined that Amy was in the office when Valerie passed out on the subway, so Dr. Herman Feldman would have done the actual killing. But did Amy have anything to do with it? Again, she wished she could meet Amy face-to-face. That way, maybe she could judge what kind of a person she was and if she were capable of conspiring in a murder.

The question of how meeting Amy could be accomplished stayed with her for the rest of the evening. She didn't mention it to Ike—he'd tell her to forget it. It was still on her mind after he'd gone home and when she fell asleep.

Liz awakened in the morning knowing exactly how she could meet Amy Baron. It was so simple, so obvious, she should have thought of it the instant she asked herself how she could do it. The Feldmans were dermatologists. She'd make an appointment to have two prominent freckles removed from her nose—the only ones that hadn't faded over the years. Makeup concealed them, so she'd never before thought of having them removed. Now they'd become her way to meet Amy Baron. Besides, she had to admit that she liked the idea of being a freckle-free bride.

Like most doctors, the Feldmans probably held some evening hours. She'd make her appointment for a time after work, on the first available date.

She called the doctors' office from her workstation.

Her spirits sank when she was told that evening appointments with both Dr. Herman and Dr. Alvin were booked solid through the first week in February and they didn't hold Saturday hours.

The woman on the phone had a warm, friendly voice. "We close at five every day except Wednesday, but even our daytime appointments are filled through January," she said, sounding regretful. "Is this urgent?"

"Not really," Liz replied. "But I'm being married in mid-February, and I want some freckles removed, and I don't want scabs on my nose on my wedding day."

"Of course you don't," the warm voice replied. "But generally the healing process takes anywhere from ten days to two weeks—sometimes longer. To be absolutely sure the areas have healed one hundred percent by your wedding day, the procedure should be done fairly soon. I'm sorry we can't accommodate you, but we can recommend another dermatologist who—" She paused abruptly and after a few seconds spoke again. "But cryosurgery doesn't take a lot of time. If you'll give me your name and phone number, I'll check with the doctors and see if one of them can work you in."

What a nice person, Liz thought, as she provided the information. When her phone rang about ten minutes later, she grabbed it.

"Hello, this is Liz Rooney."

The now-familiar warm voice responded. "Ms. Rooney, this is Amy at Dr. Feldman's office."

Amy! Momentarily stunned by the realization that the nice, warm voice belonged to the woman her imagination had involved in a murder conspiracy, Liz barely managed to acknowledge the greeting. But an instant later, her spirits bounded.

"Could you possibly come in at five this evening?" Amy Baron asked.

Quick calculation. The Feldmans' office was located in the Murray Hill area, not too far away. If she left work around a quarter to five and hopped a cab, she could make it by five. She'd clear it with Dan and tell him she'd take a short lunch break today.

"Yes, I can be there at five," she replied. "Thanks so much, Amy. How did you manage to do it?"

"When I told Dr. Herman you were going to be married, he said he'd take you after his last appointment. I was pretty sure he would. He's a sentimental softie."

This description of Dr. Herman Feldman did not jibe with Liz's mental image of him. All of a sudden the idea of the elder Feldman and his office assistant's conspiring to get rid of Valerie began to seem absurd. But she mustn't let herself be misled by a little kindness, she thought.

As far as the aftermath of the freckle removal was concerned, she knew what to expect. A college friend had had a brown spot taken off her cheek by this procedure. Tonight, when she greeted Ike at the door, she'd have two angry red welts on her nose. He'd figure it out right away. She decided to tell him about it beforehand and get it over with.

She phoned him and got as far as telling him she was going to have cryosurgery, tonight, to remove the freckles. He reacted just as she'd expected.

"Dammit, Liz—you're going to Dr. Feldman for this, aren't you?"

"Yes . . ."

"I guess you thought since you were going to have this done anyway, you might as well go to Dr. Feldman."

"Thanks for understanding."

His voice had an edge to it. "I understand, all right. You're going to do some snooping."

"I only want to observe Amy Baron."

"You think that's going to help you decide if she's capable of a murder conspiracy? I've interviewed the lady, twice, and I haven't pinned her down as a suspect."

He seemed to have temporarily departed from not discussing cases over the phone. She hastened to reply before he got back on track.

"How about my woman's angle? Remember, you told me this helped you solve the Malin case."

Ike's voice mellowed. "Sure, I remember. Okay, I guess you can't get into trouble giving Nurse Amy the once-over. Which doctor is doing the job?"

"The father."

"Good. You can size him up, too. But while you're igniting your wildfire imagination with thoughts of a conspiracy, don't forget we're not up against just one murder here. Why would the doctor and his nurse want to kill two other redheads, too?"

She laughed. "Maybe I can figure that out from my woman's angle."

"Maybe," he said. "So I'll see you at your place around six-thirty. I'll bring takeout. What'll it be?"

"Surprise me. And I have ice cream in the freezer."

"Okay." He paused. "Not that I think there's a chance you'll get into any trouble, but please be careful, Redlocks."

After filling out a form at the doctors' reception desk, Liz waited only a minute or so before she heard the familiar, warm voice.

"Elizabeth Rooney?"

Amy Baron, dark-haired, blue-eyed, slim, and pretty in a pink smock, had a smile that matched her voice. Again, Liz asked herself how such a nice person could have anything to do with a murder.

Amy led her down a corridor into a small, brightly lit room. "Just sit down over there," she said, gesturing toward an examining table. "Dr. Herman will be here in a minute." As she spoke, the door opened.

Ever since she'd seen Dr. Herman Feldman on TV, Liz had held the image in her mind of his scowling face and angry eyes. Now, as he stepped into the room, she could scarcely believe this man looking at her with such empathy could be the same person.

"So, little lady, you're going to be married soon," he said with a smile.

She quelled her startled feelings. "Yes. Thank you for letting me come in tonight."

"We're going to make sure you'll be even prettier on your wedding day than you are already," he replied. As he spoke, Amy handed him a small spotlight, which he shone onto her nose.

When, after several moments, he continued to look closely at her freckles, Liz found herself becoming nervous. *Suppose they weren't ordinary freckles but some form of skin cancer, instead?*

"Is something wrong, doctor?" she asked.

"Oh, no, nothing wrong," he assured her. "We're ready to go now. This might sting a little."

It was all over in a few minutes. Nurse Amy handed her a mirror, saying, "They'll look ugly for a while, but you'll be happy with the final result."

Dr. Feldman nodded. "Two weeks, more or less, and you'll forget they were ever there."

Liz smiled at them. "Thanks so much, both of you."

"Glad we could be of help, little lady," the doctor replied. Turning to leave, he added, "We don't see freckles on many girls your age. Generally, they fade away as the years pass. Most girls in their midtwenties who still have a few freckles also have red hair."

As the door closed behind him, Liz felt a pang of apprehension. *Could he tell that she was actually a redhead?* Suddenly, the kindly dermatologist reverted to the angry-eyed doctor she'd suspected of killing his son's girlfriend.

"Be sure and call us if you have any questions," Nurse Amy said in parting.

Could Amy tell, too? Liz's imagination took off. Her address was on the form she'd filled out earlier. Would she have to look over her shoulder every morning when she left for work? Gripped by rising panic, she managed to say good-bye to Amy and leave the building.

Outside, she saw a vacant cab coming along the street. She checked her purse to see if she had enough cash to taxi home. She didn't. Should she take a chance that Rosa or Joe would be home to borrow the fare from when she got home? Not wanting to risk it, she hurried, almost ran, to the subway station, her heart beating almost painfully, not as much from the exertion as from fear. The train pulled in a moment after she got to the platform. With a quick glance about, she boarded and remained alert all the way to Twenty-eighth Street.

Still fearful, she scurried the short distance from subway to home. Gradually, her panic began to ebb, and she started to feel a bit foolish. Chances were, when Dr. Feldman made that remark about redheads and freckles, he was simply stating an observation. If he were the killer and realized she was a redhead, would he have made that remark? Besides, would he have had time to fill up a syringe with lethal components and take off in pursuit of her? By the time she reached the Moscarettis' brownstone, she'd convinced herself that her imagination had gone haywire.

"I'm glad you warned me about your erstwhile freckles," Ike said, when he saw her. He kissed her carefully. "I hope the surgery wasn't painful."

"No, I hardly felt anything."

She decided to wait until they'd eaten before giving him the full details of her appointment with Dr. Herman Feldman. She felt pretty sure he'd laugh about her reaction to the doctor's remark concerning redheads and freckles, but if by chance he thought they contained some sinister meaning, at least he wouldn't be hungry and worried at the same time.

After dinner, when they were settled on the sofa with their coffee, she took a deep breath and told him.

"Well, he's a dermatologist," Ike said. "If there's a correlation between skin and hair, he'd know about it. What did he say, exactly? That only redheads keep their freckles into adulthood?"

Liz thought back. "No, he definitely said that *most* girls my age he'd seen whose freckles hadn't faded were redheads." She gave him a rueful look. "I guess I only half listened."

"I can understand why," he replied with a grin. "Your wildfire imagination went out of control."

"Does that mean you've ruled out Dr. Feldman?"

Ike shook his head. "None of the present persons of interest have been ruled out yet. But, with so many of them, that imagination of yours is bound to flare up like this again before the killer's caught."

"I don't want it to," she replied with a frown. "I don't want to go through anything like this ever again. This experience has taught me a lesson. I've been too deeply absorbed in the case, and the suspects, and building up far-fetched scenarios for each of them. Today, I was close to being paranoid."

Looking into his eyes, she added, "I'm making a resolution. From now on, I'm not going to allow that big parade of suspects to take over my mind. I'm going to shove them all into the background and concentrate on what's really important in my life."

"Come here—I'll help you," he said, holding out his arms.

Chapter Nine

Looking into the bathroom mirror the next morning, Liz studied the sites of her former freckles and recalled Amy Baron's words: "They'll be ugly for a while. . . ." How right she was. They looked even uglier than yesterday. For a moment she wished she'd never gotten the idea of meeting Amy face-to-face. But if she hadn't, she'd still be concentrating too much on the subway homicides case, letting it saturate her mind and stir up her imagination to the point of paranoia.

As she usually did on Saturdays, she made coffee while still in her pajamas and hopped back into her sofa bed to drink it. But, instead of turning on the TV, she reviewed the resolution she'd made last night.

Thinking less about possible suspects, motives, and scenarios wasn't going to be easy. Thoughts of Dr. Feldman and Amy had popped into her mind soon after she'd awakened, but she'd managed to switch them off and think, instead, about Ike. How wonderfully understanding he'd been last night. He didn't want her to quit her sleuthing into the subway homicides any more than she did, but he agreed with her that she'd been overly concentrated on it. Slacking off a bit might clear her mind, and she'd be better able to keep her imagination in check.

She was halfway through her coffee when Ike phoned. "I'm on my way to meet Lou and the other two on the case," he said. "We're putting in some extra time today. Have you heard a weather report this morning?"

"No, I haven't turned my TV on yet."

"No news channel? Sounds like you're really in earnest about a little backing away."

"I am. I'm severely limiting my news watching. Most of the time it's the same thing over and over, anyway. But you mentioned the weather report. Was the forecast right? Is it cooler today?"

"Yeah, the temperature's dropped. It's currently forty-two degrees."

She could hear the hesitancy in his voice, as if he were holding off telling her that cold weather might deter the killer. Jabbing a needle through heavy clothing might be too risky for him. He might botch the job.

"You don't have to cut out all talk about the subway case," she said with a laugh. "I'm not going cold turkey on this. I'm going to turn the news on in a little while."

"Good," he said. "I like the idea of your easing up a bit, but I don't want to lose my Redlocks Rooney."

After showering and dressing, Liz decided she'd held off watching the news long enough. She turned on her TV and settled down on the sofa with another mug of coffee.

The newscaster, a long-haired blond woman, was urging viewers to stay tuned for a live interview with Giles Sinclair. "Sinclair is one of the men in the life of subway murder victim, model Chloe LaFleur," she said, as if that hadn't been all over the news for the past four days.

So, reporters had finally caught up with the investment banker, Liz thought. How had he managed to elude them till now? She pictured him being picked up in a chauffeured town car and driven to his Wall Street office every morning, and being driven home in the evening, directly from the parking garage of his office building. Some die-hard newshounds must have been hanging around yesterday and spotted his car approaching the Sinclair residence. Maybe they'd surrounded it and started firing questions. Maybe they were told it was an inconvenient time but were assured they'd get an interview if they came back in the morning. However it had happened, the newscaster seemed confident that an interview was going to take place momentarily.

Although Ike had said he and Lou were close to striking Sinclair off the list of possible suspects, watching him would be interesting, Liz thought. Besides, she was curious to see what he looked like now. The photo of him in the newspaper looked as if it had been taken when he was a freshman at Harvard.

The entrance to a swanky-looking town house appeared on the screen. Moments later, the camera focused on Giles Sinclair as he stepped outside. He was a tall, handsome man in his early thirties, Liz judged, with a thick crop of light brown hair. From the tan jacket—cashmere, she felt sure—slung over the shoulders of his dark brown cable-knit sweater, to the well-polished brown loafers visible beneath his camel-colored slacks, he looked every inch high society and old money.

Liz was so intent on scrutinizing him that she didn't immediately notice the woman following a few steps behind him. Now, as he and the woman stood side by side at the entrance, she found herself studying the woman, as well.

Liz decided this had to be Sinclair's mother. She looked as if she were in her late sixties, tall, thin, with gray hair cropped in a straight, unstylish bob. Her strong, angular facial features, especially her chin, suggested she'd never been a raving beauty. Her brown sweater and skirt, houndstooth jacket, and stout leather walking shoes gave her a tweedy look synonymous with owning a country estate somewhere.

Having given Mother Sinclair the once-over, Liz waited expectantly for Giles' father to appear. A moment later he did—tall, vigorous-looking, sixty-something, silvery hair showing beneath a visored cap emblazoned with a crest that resembled a family coat of arms. She thought he looked as if he were dressed for a round of golf. The disgruntled expression on his face suggested that this interview was going to make him late for his tee time at some exclusive Westchester or New Jersey country club course.

For a minute the three of them stood there, facing the

assembled reporters and cameras in silence. Presenting a united front? Liz wondered. *Why would they feel they must do that?*

She waited for Giles' father to address the crowd. Instead, when reporters began to shout questions at Giles, his mother stepped forward, brandishing a document.

"There's no need for you to question my son," she said, her voice sounding sixty percent Katharine Hepburn and forty percent Queen Elizabeth. "Our attorneys have prepared a statement, which I shall read to you. It will answer everything."

Mrs. Sinclair seemed totally in charge, Liz thought. Gram would say she looked as if she ruled the roost. She'd probably told Giles and his father that *she* would handle this matter. And most likely she'd collaborated with the Sinclair attorneys in the wording of the statement she was about to read.

"My son had been seeing Chloe LaFleur socially for a few weeks before her death," Mrs. Sinclair began. "His interest in her was understandable." She paused, her thin lips stretching into the semblance of a smile. "What young man doesn't enjoy being seen with a very beautiful woman? But Miss LaFleur was by no means the only woman my son was seeing."

That last statement was meant to imply that Giles didn't have serious intentions about Chloe, Liz decided. She glanced at him. His face showed no reaction. She pictured his mother warning him to play it cool for the reporters—except she'd have said something more like, "Just act nonchalant."

"Furthermore, a few days before her death, Miss

LaFleur advised my son of her forthcoming marriage," Mrs. Sinclair continued. "He told me he'd wished her every happiness."

That fit right in with what Marco Denali had said in his news interview, Liz thought. It sounded as if Mrs. Sinclair had seen the interview and taken note of Marco's remarks about Chloe's letting her other boyfriends down easy.

Mrs. Sinclair read on. "Giles' father and I had never met Miss LaFleur, but from what he told us, we knew he thought of her as a friend."

She paused, lowering the document to look into the crowd of reporters and cameramen. "Although I consider it unnecessary to bring up the subject of my son's whereabouts during last Monday and Tuesday's rush hours, I will do so. Police detectives have interviewed us and members of our household staff, as well as employees of my son's firm. They are satisfied that he was nowhere near the Lexington Avenue subway when any of the homicides took place."

The way she said *Lexington Avenue subway* suggested that no Sinclair ever set foot on it. Or any other public transportation, Liz thought. And most likely the Sinclair attorneys had advised her to mention the part about police detectives being satisfied with Giles' alibi. It was almost the same as saying he was off the list of potential suspects.

Now Mrs. Sinclair wound up the so-called interview. "That will be all," she announced. She turned away from the reporters and cameras, gesturing to her husband and son to follow her into the building.

But this was not enough for the assembled newspeople. A barrage of questions followed the trio.

"Isn't it true that you disapproved of your son's relationship with Chloe LaFleur?"

"Didn't you have a young, high-society woman picked out for him to marry?"

"Weren't you afraid he'd get in too deep with Chloe?"

The questions were ignored. The Sinclairs were about to go inside, when a final query came at them. "Hey, Giles, the cat got your tongue? How come you let your mother do all the talking?"

Good question, Liz thought, watching mother, father, and son disappear into the building. The answer was obvious. Mrs. Sinclair was the dominant force in the family. Surely when Ike interviewed them, he'd noticed her autocratic tendencies. But in the light of Giles' airtight alibi, Ike had probably decided that Mrs. Sinclair's iron hand had no bearing on the case.

She recalled her speculation that a woman might have been involved in the subway homicides. Although she might not have done the actual killing, a woman might be linked to the crime in some way. Amy Baron had instilled that idea in her head, but now she found herself considering Mrs. Sinclair. Maybe she was unstable enough, mentally, to have had something to do with Chloe's murder. Ike said he was ready to scratch Giles off the potential suspect list, but had he thought about a mother wanting to get rid of a woman she considered unworthy of her son? Of course he had, she decided. Ike was a top-notch detective who considered every possibility.

At that moment, Gram phoned. "I'm all keyed up about my new Hercules," she said. "Everything's ready for him. His feeding tray is next to the fridge, and his litter box is set up in the utility room."

Exactly where his predecessor's had been, Liz thought. No need to ask where the kitten would sleep. He'd be curled up at the foot of Gram's bed, just like the old Hercules.

"I know you can't wait to get him home," Liz said. "I don't know when I'll hear from the vet saying he's ready, so why don't you grab your cat carrier and get here as soon as you can? That way, when the call comes, we can zip right over and get him."

"Oh, good idea," Gram replied. "I'll make the ten o'clock boat, and I'll hide my hair." She laughed, adding, "You won't have to worry about *this* redhead today."

Knowing that Gram would be curious about the two angry red spots on her nose, Liz told her about her appointment with Dr. Feldman.

"Good chance to find out what he's like, besides getting rid of your freckles before your wedding," Gram said.

Sophie phoned a few minutes later. She and Ralph both had the day off, and they were getting ready to drive to Yonkers for a visit with Ralph's family.

"We haven't told them yet about Ralph's going into detective training," Sophie said. "We want to be with them when we tell them. They'll want to celebrate."

Liz knew that Sophie enjoyed a wonderful relationship with Ralph's large family. She had high hopes that she'd fit in as well with Ike's. The Eichles were nowhere near as large a family as the Perillos. Ike had no brothers or sisters. He'd mentioned cousins and a couple of aunts. His parents lived upstate. She'd met them only once, when she and Ike had gone to see them after their engagement. They'd welcomed her warmly, perhaps because she'd been instrumental in patching up a longtime rift between them and Ike, and now they seemed to be okay with the reason for the rift—his choice of becoming a NYPD detective instead of an attorney like his father.

Before that visit upstate was over, Liz felt sure that Ike's parents were going to be good in-laws. They asked her to call them Doris and Walter, and when wedding plans were being discussed, they thought the idea of an ecumenical ceremony in Liz's Our Lady Queen of Peace church was a good one. That was a weight off her mind. Since the Eichles were not Catholics, she and Ike had wondered if they would object. "My family has a strong stubborn streak," Ike had told her, and she dreaded the thought of another rift between him and his parents. But ecumenical marriage ceremonies had become so commonplace in recent years, they'd gladly gone along with it.

She and Sophie talked for a few minutes. Sophie, too, had seen the TV interview with the Sinclairs, and they agreed that Mrs. Sinclair had an overpowering personality.

"If Giles didn't have an airtight alibi, I could picture his mother goading him into getting rid of Chloe," Sophie said.

"Me, too," Liz replied.

Suddenly, her thoughts switched to her successful quest to find a kitten for Gram, and she told Sophie about it. Of course Sophie remembered Hercules. He was a big part of their shared childhood memories.

"Old Herc was a neat cat," she said. "I'll never forget that throaty meow he had. You used to do a pretty good imitation of it—remember?"

"Sure I do!" Liz came out with her "*Mmmerrrow*!" adding, "See? I can still do it."

She told Sophie about the incident on the bus. "The old man sitting next to me was sure I had a cat in my handbag."

"You haven't lost your touch," Sophie replied with a laugh.

"And I hope I haven't lost my common sense," Liz said. "Wait till you hear this!" She gave a brief but complete rundown of the Dr. Feldman incident.

"Wow," Sophie replied. "Sounds like you let your imagination run away with you."

"Yes, I did, and I'm making sure something like that never happens again." She told Sophie about her resolution, adding, "With Ike working weekends and a lot of nights, it's going to be easier said than done."

"Yeah, that leaves you with nothing much to do but think about the case all by yourself. You need a break. If I wasn't going to Yonkers today, we could get together. Sure, we'd discuss the subway homicides, but we always have lots of other things to talk about."

Liz could hear Ralph's voice in the background. "I

know Ralph wants to get going, so I'll say good-bye," she replied.

"Bye." Sophie said. "We'll get together soon."

After Liz hung up the phone, she launched into her Saturday-morning housekeeping routine. By the time that was done, she realized Gram would be arriving soon. Also, someone would be calling from Dr. Jurgens' office.

At that moment, as if on cue, her phone rang. It was the vet's receptionist, calling to tell her the kitten was ready.

"Thanks, Gail," Liz said. "I'll pick him up shortly."

Chapter Ten

Gram arrived about ten minutes later, cat carrier in hand, all smiles, wearing decidedly wintry pants and jacket because of the drop in temperature. She'd bundled her hair under a brown beret.

"Just in case the subway killer is riding the trains today, I wanted to make sure I didn't remind him of his mean old redheaded English teacher," she joked.

Glancing at Liz's nose, she added, "You had a crop of freckles when you were kid, but I thought they'd all pretty much faded by now. I never noticed those two."

"I kept them covered with makeup."

"Well, you won't have to fuss with that anymore. Did you get any ideas about the case when you were at the dermatologists'?"

"Nothing much."

Not exactly the truth, Liz thought, but by now she wanted to forget about the wild imaginings that had thrown her into a panic. Talking about it would make her feel even more foolish.

Because it was cold and windy, they took the subway to Thirty-third Street and walked the short distance from there to Dr. Jurgens' office.

"We'll get a cab after we pick up Hercules," Gram said. "He might be frightened on the subway. And I'll just drop you off on my way to the ferry."

"I know you want to get him home as soon as possible," Liz replied, as they entered the veterinarian's waiting room.

Both the dogs' side and the cats' were crowded with pets and their owners—some waiting to see Dr. Jurgens, others on their way out with dogs on leashes and cats in carriers.

The receptionist recognized Liz. "You've come for the black kitten, haven't you?" she asked. She reached for her phone. "I'll tell Paula you're here."

Gram was settling the bill when Paula appeared. She glanced at Liz's freckle sites, saying, "Hello, Liz. I see you've had skin surgery. I had a mole taken off my neck last year. Cost me a fortune. I think the doctor knew I could afford it, and he overcharged me."

While Liz was thinking this was an odd remark, Paula said she'd take them to the cages where the kitten was waiting. "If you need a carrier, we can lend you one," she added.

Gram turned away from the reception desk, saying, "Thanks, but I have one."

After Liz introduced them, Paula said, "The black

kitten is going to be a wonderful pet for you, Mrs. McGowan. Let's go back to the cages, and you can get acquainted with him before you take him home."

Paula had a warm, friendly way about her, Liz thought, as they walked down a corridor. Inside the room where the cats were caged, Paula paused to tap her hand on each grating and speak the pet's name.

When she brought Hercules the Second out of his cage, Liz wished she could have snapped a photo. But even without one, she knew she'd never forget the happy look on Gram's face.

"Do you have a cat, Paula?" Liz asked, as Gram cuddled the kitten.

Paula's face clouded. "I had one, but then I got a dog who hates cats. I'd had dogs and cats together as pets before, and they got along fine, so I thought Brutus would at least grow to tolerate Tippy, but it turned out he's one of those dogs who'll never adjust to living with a cat. He barked at her nonstop, so I found another home for Tippy."

"Oh, too bad," Liz said.

"Yes, it was, especially since that didn't totally solve the barking problem. Brutus still barks too much. He barks at everyone who comes to the door, even people he knows, like the man from the dog-walking service."

"What breed is he?" Liz asked.

"A Doberman pinscher. Purebred. You can hear his bark for blocks. Before I got rid of Tippy, all my neighbors complained constantly, and my landlord was ready to throw me out. I had to make a choice. I got Brutus not only for a pet but also a watchdog, because I have valuable jewelry and furs and other items, and even though I live in an upscale area in a supposedly secure building, you never know. So Tippy had to go. I still miss her."

A purebred Doberman, a professional dog-walker, an upscale address, jewels, furs . . . All that plus her taking cabs everywhere made Liz decide that Paula was not dependent on her salary as a veterinarian's assistant. Most likely, she didn't have to work at all.

All that was not lost on Gram, either. Never one to withhold her thoughts or opinions, she spoke up. "Sounds like you're working here because you love animals."

Paula nodded. "Yes, I absolutely adore them. That's why I took this job. I guess you figured out I don't have to depend on my salary." She smiled. "Where I come from, the Rubiks are like the Rockefellers."

Hearing that statement, Liz felt a bit startled. If the Rooneys were like the Rockefellers, would *she* talk about it so freely?

Paula was talking on. "I inherited a bundle. That's when I decided to come to New York. Even though I was having a ball, making new friends, seeing all the Broadway shows, dining in all the best restaurants, I missed having a bunch of animals around. I grew up with all kinds of animals, from hamsters to horses, so even after I got Brutus and Tippy, I didn't feel content until I started working here."

Paula's explanation could have done without the

---

constant reminders of her family's wealth, Liz thought. "Well, we should be getting the kitten home," she said, hoping to put an end to it.

Gram cast her a look that seemed to say she, too, had heard enough about Paula's money. "Yes, we should be going," she said, easing Hercules into the cat carrier.

Paula walked down the corridor with them. "Of course, you'll be taking your kitten to a vet out on Staten Island," she said to Gram. "So I won't be seeing you anymore. I wish you the best of luck with him."

At the entrance, she turned to Liz, saying, "But I hope you and I can get together sometime, Liz. I noticed you're wearing an engagement ring, and that means your time is pretty well taken up by your fiancé, but would you be free on an occasional Sunday afternoon for a movie or something?"

With Ike working extra hard on the subway homicides, she'd often be at loose ends on weekends. With so much free time on her hands, she might find it difficult to stick to her resolution.

"Sure, Paula." Having already told all there was to know about her financial situation, it wasn't likely Paula would repeat it, she decided.

"Good." Paula replied, looking pleased. "We have your home phone number on record. I'll give you a call soon."

"Oh, I see a taxi," Gram said. "We'd better get out there and flag it down."

In the cab, she looked at Liz with a shake of her head. "I hope you're not thinking of taking up with that bragging rich girl."

"I know she talked too much about her money, but otherwise I like her. I might get together with her once in a while."

"Well, I can't choose your friends for you," Gram said.

"Taking in a movie with her now and then doesn't mean we're going to be bosom buddies," Liz replied. "Ike's going to be tied up working overtime, and I'll have time on my hands. Besides . . ."

She told Gram about her panic attack and her resolution.

Gram gave her an understanding nod and a pat on the hand. "You need to fill up the time when Ike's working," she said. "With Sophie married now, the two of you don't get together like you used to. You need an extra friend. Well, this Paula seems like a nice girl, even if she brags too much. She's certainly very attractive."

"Yes, and how about her hair?" Liz asked. "Did you ever see such a gorgeous shade of red?"

Gram laughed. "That color came straight out of a bottle."

Liz looked at her in surprise. "How can you be so sure?"

"I've seen enough dye jobs at Nick's Crowning Glory, including my own, to recognize one when I see one," Gram replied. "After that maniac started killing pretty young redheads on the subway, she should have gone back to her own color. There are products that strip the dye off, right down to the natural."

"Maybe she thinks her own color is too blah. She knows she looks great as a redhead, and, besides, she thinks she's safe because she never rides the subway. She takes cabs everywhere."

Gram gave a snort. "Oh, I forgot. She's like one of the Rockefellers."

At that moment, the taxi stopped in front of the Moscarettis' brownstone. Gram patted Liz's hand again, saying, "I shouldn't have made that remark. Except for her bragging, this Paula seems like a very nice girl, and I'm glad you've found a new friend. She's not another Sophie, though."

"There'll never be another Sophie," Liz replied, giving Gram a good-bye kiss.

Sophie was going to get a laugh out of Paula's discourse on the Rubik billions, she thought, as the cab pulled away.

Chapter Eleven

On the way up the stairs to her apartment, Liz thought about her resolution. It was going pretty well. Gram and her kitten had dominated her mind most of the morning. Diverting herself had worked well. Getting together with Paula would provide useful diversion when Ike was tied up.

But the instant she stepped inside her apartment, it was as if all the possible suspects were there, waiting for her. *Waiting to put wild schemes into my head and send my imagination flaring.*

No more of that, she told herself. No more ideas about meeting thcm face-to-face and letting her imagination run wild because of some chance remark. Instead of turning the TV to a news channel, she made a grilled cheese sandwich for lunch, heated up coffee left over from breakfast, put it all on a tray, and settled herself on the sofa.

105

Her fingers itched to turn on the TV. What if something big had happened, such as another subway murder? She willed herself to wait until she'd eaten her
lunch before watching the news. If anything new had
developed in the case, it would be rerun over and over.

She'd just finished eating when a knock sounded on
her door, followed by Rosa's voice. "The mail came,
dearie. I brought yours up."

When Liz opened the door, Rosa handed her two en-
velopes. "You got your phone bill and a letter with an
upstate postmark," Rosa said. "At first I thought it was
from Ike's parents, but the address is different. Must be
from some other relative."

"Thanks, Rosa." Liz had become accustomed to this
daily scrutiny of her mail and grown too fond of Rosa
to be annoyed.

"I know you want to read the letter right away, but I
have something to tell you before I go," Rosa said. "I
want to start looking for a good tenant for your apartment, so I put an ad in the newspaper saying I have a
studio apartment for rent, available March first. If you're
at work when someone wants to come and look at it,
would you mind if I let them see it?"

"Of course I wouldn't mind, Rosa."

"Thanks. I want to take my time and make sure we
get a nice tenant." She smiled. "Someone as nice as you.
Well, I'll be going so you can read your letter."

Liz looked at the name on the envelope. *Hilda Eichle.*
Ike's mother's name was Doris. And, as Rosa had pointed
out, the return address was different. Ike had told her his

grandparents were dead. This Hilda Eichle might be an aunt or a cousin, she thought, opening the envelope.

My dear Miss Elizabeth Rooney, the letter began. Not exactly a warm start. Liz got the feeling the rest of it would be just as chilly.

It has come to my attention that you and my great-nephew, George, are planning to be married in February in a Roman Catholic church with a Roman Catholic priest and a Lutheran pastor officiating. This is unacceptable to me.

Liz could not believe what she was reading. Who did this great-aunt think she was, objecting to Ike's wedding plans when his parents were okay with them? She resisted the urge to tear the letter into shreds. Instead, she read on.

No member of the Eichle family has ever been married in a Roman Catholic church. George and his parents are aware of this, and I am profoundly displeased with them and greatly disturbed by this breach of family tradition. Unless you and my great-nephew agree to be married in a Protestant church by a Protestant clergyman, and no Catholic priest participating, I intend to cut George and his parents out of my will and leave all my money and property to charity.

The letter was signed simply *Hilda Eichle.*

Liz stared at the signature. Ike had never mentioned a Great-aunt Hilda. Evidently they weren't close, and that wasn't surprising. She sounded like a bigoted old harridan who believed she could dictate to family members via her bankroll. Was she Ike's maiden aunt by blood, or had she married into the Eichle family? Either way, where had her money come from, if she actually had any?

As a great-aunt, possibly she was in her eighties, or even older, but her handwriting was strong and legible, and the language of the letter was not the rambling of someone out of her senses, who believed she was wealthy but wasn't.

She decided to call Ike. This was something she avoided doing when he was working. He'd be calling her as usual sometime during the afternoon, but she needed to talk to him about this now. If it were true that this great-aunt had a lot of money, she didn't want to be responsible for Ike and his parents losing out on a sizable inheritance. Something had to be worked out, she thought, as she punched Ike's number.

When he answered, he sounded as if he knew she wouldn't be calling him unless she had something important to tell him. "Liz. What's up?"

"Can you spare a few minutes?" she asked.

"Sure. Is something wrong? You sound upset."

"I guess I am, a little, but before I explain, please tell me about your Great-aunt Hilda."

"She's my grandfather's sister. Never married. Kind of a recluse. How did you know I . . ."

"I just got a letter from her. She says if we get married in a Catholic church, she's going to disinherit you and your parents and leave everything she has to charity."

She paused with the faint hope he'd laugh and say to forget it—Aunt Hilda's wealth existed solely in her mind.

Instead, he gave a groan. "I should have known the old girl would try to pull something like this."

"Is it true she has a lot of money?"

"Yeah, she's loaded. It would have been nice for us to get some of it someday, but I'm not putting up with this. Don't worry about it, Liz. Just ignore the letter."

"But what about your parents? She said she'd cut them off, too."

"Since her beef is mainly with me, maybe I can get her to reconsider involving my parents. They're financially comfortable, but with my Dad retiring soon, they could use extra money down the road. But I'm telling you, Liz, I won't stand for her threatening you."

"I could rethink our wedding plans," Liz said. "Maybe we could be married in Gram's house."

She could almost see Ike shaking his head. "Aunt Hilda's too stubborn to compromise. She won't settle for anything but a Protestant church and a Protestant clergyman. Soon as I get a breather on this case, I'll go up to Syracuse and try to reason with her. Maybe I can talk her out of disinheriting my folks. No telling when I can get away, but there'll be a break sooner or later."

An idea sprang into Liz's mind. She needed a diversion from her overactive imagination, and Ike's stubborn old aunt needed someone to set her straight. "For your parents' sake, we should get this settled as soon as possible. How would it be if *I* made the trip up to see her? Maybe I could reason with her."

Ike laughed. "I know you could charm the birds right off the trees, but you'd be dealing with an old crow."

"I'd make it clear I didn't come to see her on your behalf. I'd try to persuade her to keep your parents in her will. I'd tell her your parents shouldn't be disinherited just because you and I will not change our plans. The sooner this is settled, the better. I'd like to make the trip right away."

Ike was silent for a few moments. "You're a real sweetheart to think of doing this," he said. "It's a long haul for such a long shot, but if you really want to do it, I guess it's worth a try."

"I've never been to Syracuse, but it can't be much more than a three-hour drive," she said. "I'll borrow Gram's car and leave tomorrow morning."

Ike shook his head. "Since you'll be going alone, I'd rather you flew. The weather upstate can turn bad this time of year, and I don't want you driving on icy roads. Besides, leaving tomorrow by car wouldn't give you enough time to see Aunt Hilda and get back in time for work on Monday. If you can get a flight out sometime after six tonight, I'll drive you to the airport."

"I guess you're right," she replied.

"I'll call my folks and arrange for you to stay overnight with them," he said.

"Good. I'll have plenty of time tomorrow to visit your aunt and get an evening flight back."

"They'll be delighted you're coming, and they'll want to meet your plane. I'll phone you after I've talked with them. Go ahead and make your reservation—and of course the plane fare's on me."

Later, while Ike drove her to catch a flight out of LaGuardia, he told her he'd talked his parents.

"They both appreciate what you're trying to do, and they're looking forward to seeing you. Aunt Hilda sent them the same kind of letter she sent you. They're outraged—especially my mother. She says the old girl's spoiling what should be one of the happiest times in your life."

"Are you sure they don't they blame me for putting their inheritance in jeopardy?" Liz asked. "I can't help feeling this is all my fault."

"Your fault? Because you happen to be Catholic? No way."

"Maybe your aunt would agree to a compromise. What if we got married at City Hall and had a Catholic marriage later?"

"That wouldn't work. You can bet Aunt Hilda will be keeping a sharp eye on the proceedings. She'd find out about the Catholic wedding. Besides, she wouldn't approve of City Hall. She wants us to be married in a Protestant church by a Protestant clergyman."

Liz held back a sigh of resignation. "If I can't get anywhere with your aunt, then maybe that's what we should do."

Ike shook his head with vehemence. "I can't let you do that. We'll be married in your church, as planned. Believe me, my folks are not blaming you for this. They're as angry as I am about Aunt Hilda's bigotry."

She cast him a grateful look. "How did she get that way, do you know?"

He nodded. "According to family talk, during her last year at college, she and a Catholic man were deeply in love, but the romance went sour because of their different religions, I don't know the details, but evidently it left her bitter and prejudiced."

"So that's why she never married," Liz said.

"I assume so. She got a job as a real estate agent and then started investing and dealing. She must have been a smart cookie. That's how she got all her money."

"I hope I can persuade her to let your parents off the hook. If I can't, I'll feel guilty the rest of my life, and your parents might grow to resent me for depriving them of their inheritance."

Ike shook his head. "I've heard Dad say, more than once, that nobody should go through life counting on somebody else's money."

"Sounds like something Pop would say," Liz replied. The thought cheered her. If Aunt Hilda proved to be too hateful and bitter to reason with, if she refused to compromise and allow Ike's parents to remain her beneficiaries, at least there was a chance his father would not hold it against her.

She heard Ike give a low chuckle. "Are you sure you want to marry into a family where there's such a strong stubborn streak? First my folks didn't speak to me for five years because I didn't take up law. Now there's my great-aunt standing firm about changing our marriage plans." He cast her a grin. "And how about when I was so dead set against your interest in following homicides?"

"If you're trying to talk me out of marrying you, lotsa luck," she replied. "I have a stubborn streak of my own."

Chapter Twelve

"There it is, Berwyck Manor Retirement Community, just ahead on the right," Ike's father, Walter, said, slowing his Buick LeSabre on a quiet suburban Syracuse street.

Liz gazed at the complex of stately brick buildings set back beyond an open gateway and an expanse of green lawn and trees. The few misgivings she'd had on the flight last night had dwindled. From the moment Ike's parents had picked her up at the airport, she had felt confident she'd done the right thing in making this trip. A few weeks ago, when Ike had taken her to meet them, she'd felt very comfortable with them. This time they were every bit as warm and welcoming. On the drive from the airport to the Eichle home last night, it was evident they didn't blame her for the threatened loss of their inheritance.

Only a few minutes after they picked her up at the

airport, Ike's mother, Doris, had said, "Forgive me for being curious, Liz, but may I ask you a personal question?"

"Of course," Liz replied. Was she going to inquire about the spots on her nose? They hadn't healed enough yet to be covered with makeup.

"What did you do to your hair?" Doris asked. "I've been telling all our friends about our beautiful red-haired future daughter-in-law."

Pleasantly surprised, Liz was about to explain, when Walter spoke up. "I'll bet she dyed it to keep from becoming another victim of that serial killer who's going after red-haired women on the New York subway—right, Liz?"

"Right. But I'm hoping the case will be solved and I'll be a redhead again before the wedding," Liz replied. "There's something that strips the dye out of the hair and restores the natural color. I'll use it as soon as the killer is caught."

"Those horrible murders!" Doris exclaimed. "We were very worried about you when we heard about them, but when we phoned George, he said the two of you had thought of a way to keep you out of danger."

"Dying your hair was a clever move," Walter said.

Liz took great pleasure in telling them it had been Ike's idea.

Now, as Walter turned the Buick through brick gateposts onto the grounds of Berwyck Manor, she began to feel a bit nervous. Although they'd discussed everything in advance, she needed reassurance.

"Are you sure you don't want to go in with me to see her?" she asked. "Won't she wonder why you didn't come for a visit?"

"Under the circumstances, it's best that we just drop you off," Walter replied. "When you're ready to leave, give us a call, and when we come for you, we'll have our visit with her."

"Shouldn't we have let her know I'm coming? Suppose she went to church or something?"

"If we told her you were coming, she'd have some excuse not to see you," Doris said. "And don't worry about her not being there. She rarely goes anywhere, not even to church. If she wants to attend a Sunday service, there's a chaplain and a nondenominational chapel on the premises."

For someone who didn't attend any church herself, Aunt Hilda had some nerve interfering in her great nephew's Catholic church wedding, Liz thought.

Walter braked the Buick at the pillared and porticoed main entrance and looked at Liz with a smile. "We appreciate your trying to turn things around for us."

"Yes, we do," Doris added. "But please, Liz dear, don't feel bad if it doesn't happen. We're not counting on it."

"Let's hope I can pull it off," Liz said.

In the beautifully furnished lobby of Berwyck Manor, she gave her name to a receptionist and said she'd come to visit Miss Hilda Eichle. "I hope she's here—she's not expecting me," she added.

The receptionist picked up a phone, saying, "I'm sure she's in her apartment. She's usually there except at mealtime."

Doubtful thoughts crowded Liz's mind. Would Aunt Hilda agree to receive the young woman to whom she'd written such a scathing letter? She bolstered her spirits with the hope that Aunt Hilda might be curious. She might want to size up someone who'd present herself immediately after getting such a poisonous message.

"Ms. Rooney . . ." The receptionist's voice penetrated her thoughts. "Miss Eichle is in her apartment. She asked me to send you up."

That could be a good sign, Liz thought. At least Aunt Hilda hadn't run her off, sight unseen.

She got directions to the apartment and took an elevator to the second floor. As she walked along a plushly carpeted corridor past walls lined with handsomely framed art reproductions, the ongoing atmosphere of opulence continued to impress her. This place was definitely designed for wealthy retirees. When Ike's parents were ready for a retirement complex, they deserved to live in a place like this, she thought. Ike had told her they were fairly well off—*comfortable* was how he'd described it—but someday, when they were ready to give up the hassles of living in their own home, would inflation have diminished their retirement income? Could they afford an upscale haven like this, or would they have to settle for some dreary, mediocre place to live out their declining years?

It's up to me. Pausing at the door to apartment 2-E, she reached for the ornate brass knocker.

She'd only knocked once when she heard a peevish voice from the other side of the door. "I'm coming, I'm coming. . . ." Moments later the door opened, and she found herself face-to-face with a small, wiry woman whose snow-white hair was tied back in sort of an octogenarian-style ponytail and fastened with a black ribbon. She had on a black dress that looked as if it had come with a hefty price tag during the Reagan presidency, plus black hose and black flat-heeled pumps.

Penetrating dark eyes beneath pepper-and-salt eyebrows unabashedly scrutinized Liz. "So you're the girl who's going to make a Roman Catholic out of my great-nephew," she snapped. "Why have you come here? To try to talk me out of disinheriting him so the two of you can enjoy my money after I'm gone?"

Liz felt her Irish temper stirring. Ask a rude question, and get a rude answer, she thought. "I have no intentions of making a Catholic out of anyone, least of all your great-nephew," she retorted. "Neither he nor I give a hoot about your precious money. If you'll do me the courtesy of asking me in, I'll tell you why I'm here."

She wouldn't have been surprised to have the door slammed in her face, but she was counting on an old woman's curiosity.

She detected a glimmer of surprise in the dark, penetrating eyes. The door swung open. "With a muttered, "Come in," Aunt Hilda led her through a small foyer into a large room dimmed by green damask window draperies. It could only be described as a Victorian parlor. All these antiques must have been passed down through generations of Eichles, Liz thought, gazing around at the velvet-and-rosewood chairs and settees, the clutter of bibelots atop marble-topped tables and chests, and the rug that looked as if it had once graced a Persian palace.

"Well, out with it," Aunt Hilda said, sitting down on a red velvet love seat and motioning for Liz to sit in a nearby green chair.

Liz sensed she was being physically appraised and felt thankful she'd worn the tan skirt suit and brown topcoat she'd bought last payday. Along with her brown turtleneck sweater and brown leather boots, she felt very well dressed. When a woman knew she looked good, she felt confident, and if she'd ever needed confidence, it was now.

As an indication she intended to stay for more than a few minutes, she took off her topcoat and draped it over the back of her chair. After a deep, calming breath, she gathered what she hoped were the right words. "Your great-nephew and I are going ahead with our plans to be married in the church I've attended since I was a child," she said. "As I told you, I have no intention of changing his religion. I couldn't do that even if I wanted to. Ike . . . uh, George . . . is no namby-pamby milksop. That's why he won't knuckle under to your demands. We both realize the money you would have left him might make our lives easier someday, but—"

Aunt Hilda bristled. "It would do far more than that. I haven't got too many years left. You'd have money when you're young enough to enjoy it. You'd never have to worry about paying for your children's educations.

You'd—" She stopped short. "If you're serious about not wanting my money, why did you come to see me?"

"I came on behalf of your great-nephew's parents. It's not fair to cut them out of your will because of something they're not responsible for."

Aunt Hilda's pepper-and-salt eyebrows came together in a scowl. "Doris and Walter should have disapproved. They should have told you they won't attend your wedding if it's held in a Roman Catholic church."

"Why should they do that?" Liz asked.

Aunt Hilda almost spat out her reply. "Because no member of the Eichle family has ever been married by a Roman Catholic priest in a Roman Catholic church."

"It's going to be an ecumenical service," Liz said. "We thought that would please Ike's parents, and apparently it did."

"Well, it doesn't please *me,*" Aunt Hilda barked. She shot Liz a semi-glare. "Why do you keep saying 'Ike'? Is that what you call my great-nephew instead of George?"

"Yes. All his friends call him Ike."

Aunt Hilda's facial expression suddenly went from irate to pensive. "I never knew that," she replied. "I wasn't close to George when he was growing up, and then, of course, when he graduated from college, he went to New York and became a policeman."

Liz could not hold back a smile. "And now he's just about the best detective in the NYPD."

"Eichle . . . Ike," Aunt Hilda said, cocking her head as if she were mulling the names over in her mind. "I like it. Reminds me of General Dwight Eisenhower. They called *him* Ike, too. Fine man. He won the war for us, and he was elected president twice."

Liz sensed a spark of warmth and hastened to take advantage of it. "Like General Ike Eisenhower, your great-nephew Ike Eichle is no namby-pamby. He—"

Aunt Hilda interrupted. "You used that expression, 'namby-pamby,' before. You also said 'milksop.' I haven't heard anyone use those words in years."

Liz nodded. "*Wimp* is the word these days."

"Where did you pick up those old-fashioned words?"

"From my grandmother. We talk a lot."

"I take it you're close to her."

"Yes, very. I've always been close to Gram. And now that my parents have moved to Florida, we're even closer."

A sardonic smile played about Aunt Hilda's thin mouth. "You expect to inherit money from your grandmother. That's why you're kowtowing to her, and that's why you don't need *my* money."

Liz gulped back a retort that might have blown her whole mission. "You could not be more mistaken," she managed to say.

Aunt Hilda went silent for a few moments. When she spoke, she sounded almost angry. "What does a girl your age find to talk about with an old woman?"

"Oh, everything, but especially murder cases. I'm into following sensational homicides and trying to come up with clues. Gram likes to do that, too. She's very clever at putting things together. For the past week we've been trying to figure out who killed those three women on the New York subway. I guess you heard about that on TV."

"I read about it in the newspaper," Aunt Hilda replied. "I never watch television. Nothing but garbage on it." She paused, as if reflecting. "Those three women who were murdered on the subway—they all had red hair, didn't they?"

"Yes," Liz replied. *Should I go into details? Should I say I, too, had red hair and that Ike suggested I dye it?*

Aunt Hilda's dark eyes scrutinized her. "When Doris and Walter told me their son was engaged to be married, they showed me a snapshot of you. Your hair was red, but it's brown now. Did you dye it to protect yourself from the subway killer?"

Liz laughed, nodding. "You're as good as Gram at picking up on things."

Aunt Hilda almost smiled. "I've always been sharp, if I do say so myself, but these days nobody realizes it."

She was comparing her own reclusive existence with Gram's full life, Liz thought. "It didn't take *me* long to realize it," she said.

Aunt Hilda cast her a penetrating glance, then consulted a small gold watch dangling from a chain around her neck. Rising, she went to a breakfront chest.

"I always have a glass of wine at this timc of day," she said, opening the chest. "Will you join me?"

Liz was as startled by the question as she was by the array of bottles, decanters, glasses, and goblets. "Yes, thank you," she managed to say.

"I'd be pleased if you'd have lunch with me, too. The dining room opens in about an hour," Aunt Hilda said, handing Liz a stemmed glass of red wine. Before Liz could accept the invitation, she frowned. "Or do you expect Doris and Walter to pick you up momentarily?"

"No. I'm going to call them when I'm ready to leave, so I'd enjoy having lunch with you," Liz replied. "They said they'd stay for a visit when they come to pick me up."

"In and out like jackrabbits, as usual," Aunt Hilda muttered, taking a drink of her wine.

"Have you ever asked *them* to have a glass of wine with you or invited them for lunch?" Liz asked.

"They wouldn't be interested. The only reason they ever visit is because of the money they're going to get when I die."

"That's not true," Liz replied. "When they come back for me, they're paying you a visit, even though you've made it clear they're not going to inherit any of your money because of Ike and me getting married in my church."

Aunt Hilda took several sips from her wineglass. "That's because they think you could change my mind," she said. "That's why they sent you here, isn't it?"

"No, coming here was my own idea," Liz replied, as calmly as possible. "I was hoping you'd reconsider your ultimatum as far as Ike's parents are concerned. The money you would have left them would make life easier for them when they grow old. They should not be penalized for something Ike and I have decided to do."

"It's not too late," Aunt Hilda said. "If Doris and Walter want the money I intended to leave them, they should object to their son marrying in the Roman Catholic Church and refuse to attend the wedding."

Liz's dander was up, perhaps urged on by the heady wine. "Do you want them to pretend they disapprove in order to get your money?"

Aunt Hilda looked confused. Liz hoped she was thinking this would leave her closer to defeat than victory.

During the brief silence, Liz struggled to hold back the words she'd been longing to say, but they came out anyway. "You're so hung up on your wealth and the power you think it gives you, you can't think of anything else. Didn't it ever occur to you that your relatives could be fond of you even if you didn't have a dime? I'd rather have what my grandmother and I have between us than a potful of money."

Aunt Hilda drained her wineglass and stared at Liz for a few moments. Her reply was barely audible. "I wasn't always like this."

Liz hesitated before asking, "Do you want to talk about it?" *Would the question offend Aunt Hilda and put an unsuccessful end to the visit?*

It didn't. Instead, Aunt Hilda refilled her own wineglass and added more to what Liz had left in hers. After taking a generous sip, she leveled her eyes on Liz. "If things had been different, I could have had a granddaughter," she said. "We could have been as close as you and your grandmother." Her eyes took on a faraway expression.

Liz felt greatly encouraged. Aunt Hilda seemed close to talking about her blighted romance. This could mean she was warming up—perhaps even enough to change her mind about cutting Doris and Walter out of her will.

"Different?" she asked.

The words came out in a torrent. "Yes. My college sweetheart and I were head over heels in love. After graduation, we wanted to get married, but he came from a strict Roman Catholic family, and they disapproved because I was a Protestant. We told them we'd follow the approved procedure for mixed-marriage couples—be married by a Catholic priest in the priest's office. This was all right with *my* family, but his family insisted I convert to Catholicism and be married in their church. They would not budge. I didn't believe I could ever be a good Catholic, so I refused to convert. I thought my sweetheart loved me enough to stand up to his family, but . . ." Her voice trailed off.

Liz felt a deep sense of compassion. Aunt Hilda didn't have to say her college sweetheart was the only man she had ever loved, or that this heartbreak had left her with an abiding hatred for the Catholic Church. Yes, things would have been different for Aunt Hilda if her sweetheart had only had the gumption to defy his family.

A sudden thought struck her at that moment, forming into words she couldn't hold back. "Thank heaven your great-nephew, Ike, isn't like that."

Aunt Hilda looked startled. Her eyes met Liz's in a penetrating glare. Her voice, harsh with anger, stated, "What you're really saying is that the only man I ever loved was a . . . . *wimp.*"

Liz wished she could take back her hurtful words.

She realized she'd tarnished Aunt Hilda's image of her long-ago sweetheart, her one and only love. False as the image was, Aunt Hilda had cherished it for more than half a century. Just when Aunt Hilda seemed to be softening, the *wimp* word had blown it. Ike's parents would have to do without a cushion of cash in their old age.

She tried to think of something to say—something that would express her regret—but it was too late. Glowering, Aunt Hilda had already risen from the red velvet love seat and was gesturing toward the door.

"It's time you were leaving," she said. "You can call Doris and Walter from the lobby and tell them to pick you up. And you can also tell them to forget about visiting me today—or any other day, for that matter."

Chapter Thirteen

"**I** feel terrible," Liz said, as she and Ike walked to the LaGuardia Airport parking area. "I know I was getting through to her, and then I blew it."

"Don't beat yourself up," Ike replied. "My folks phoned me after they took you to the airport. They weren't surprised it didn't work out."

When they got to the Taurus, he gave her a hug. "Cheer up. The trip wasn't a total loss. My folks enjoyed seeing you and getting to know you better. My mother said she feels this has brought us all closer together."

What great in-laws Doris and Walter were going to be, Liz thought. "They're such good sports," she said. "I'm sure they were disappointed."

"Maybe, but they knew it would take a miracle worker to break through Aunt Hilda's stubbornness," Ike replied. "Thanks for trying to accomplish the impossible."

In the car he drew her close and kissed her. "Besides you and my parents getting closer, I've just thought of something else that made this trip worthwhile," he said. "It got your mind off all those potential murder suspects and gave your imagination a good rest."

She felt herself brightening. "Yes, it did. It was just what I needed. Now I'm ready to restart, but there'll be no more schemes for face-to-face encounters."

He started the car and flashed a grin. "Promise?"

"Absolutely."

"That's good. This case is tough enough without my having to worry about you."

"How's it going? Anything new in the past twenty-four hours?"

"Nope."

He sounded discouraged, Liz thought. "It hasn't been a week yet since the first redhead was brought into the morgue," she reminded him.

She'd barely spoken the words when she remembered that many of his cases were further along or solved in less than a week. On this one he wasn't even close to making an arrest.

She held back a sigh of regret. With all her intense concentration on the case, she hadn't stumbled across anything that might help him. But now that she'd resolved to lighten up and she'd sworn off schemes such as the one involving Dr. Feldman and Nurse Amy, she could put her mind to work in a more rational way. Even one small, seemingly unrelated thing might lead her to a piece of the puzzle.

Ike's voice broke into her thoughts. "You must be hungry," he said. "I know you didn't get any dinner on that short flight. Shall we stop for takeout?"

"Yes, let's pick up a pizza."

"I wish I could spend the whole evening with you, but I'll have to take off after we eat," he said.

She quelled her disappointment. This was how it would be until the subway homicides case was solved.

After they'd eaten and Ike had gone, Liz called Gram to get an update on the new Hercules.

"He's settled in and getting very affectionate," Gram reported. "I can't thank you enough for the trouble you took getting him for me. You've made me very happy."

"Well, I'm happy, too, knowing it's working out so well," Liz replied. She was about to tell Gram about her trip upstate and Aunt Hilda, but Gram said she was getting ready to go out to a neighbor's house for an evening of bridge.

"I don't want to be late, so I'll have to leave right now," she said.

They said good-bye. Liz checked her watch. Sophie should be home from Yonkers by now. She put in the call, and Sophie answered.

"Liz! I was just going to phone you!"

"Hi. Did you have a good visit with Ralph's family?"

"We had a great time, but I've been thinking about you. What did you do Saturday night and all day today, with Ike working? No more wild schemes, I hope. You know that old saying, 'Satan will find mischief for idle hands to do.' "

"Satan had nothing to do with how I spent my time," Liz said. "But listen to this. . . ."

Sophie must have been stricken speechless, Liz thought. She didn't interrupt or say a word until the entire tale was told. If it hadn't been for a number of denunciatory grunts, Liz might have thought the phone connection had been cut off.

"What a crotchety old lady!" Sophie exclaimed, when Liz wound up her discourse. "But Ike's right—the trip wasn't a total loss. Sounds like his folks have grown very fond of you. Have you told Gram about all this?"

"Not yet. I phoned her earlier to see how the kitten's doing, but she was on her way out to play bridge, so I didn't get around to it."

"How's she getting along with Hercules Junior?"

"Great." Thinking of Hercules made Liz think of Paula Rubik. "Oh, here's something you'll get a laugh out of," she said. "It's about a woman who works at the vet's where I got Gram's kitten."

She related Paula's remarks about her family's wealth.

"I can't believe this woman actually compared her family to the Rockefellers," Sophie said, after she stopped laughing. "She reminds me of that girl in college who was always bragging about being rich. Million Dollar Millie, we called her—remember?"

"I remember her now. I don't know why I didn't think of her when I was listening to Paula. But except for the bragging, Paula's okay. She wants us to get together for a movie some Sunday afternoon. With Ike putting in extra time on weekends, I think I will."

"Good. That will fill the void and keep you from thinking up ways to get close to other possible suspects." Sophie paused, then laughed. "But, come to think of it, getting close to Marco Denali wouldn't be so bad."

Liz laughed, too. "I should have chosen the Dean Martin look-alike instead of Dr. Feldman to get up close and personal with."

After they said good-bye, Liz turned her TV on to a news channel. She hadn't watched any news about the subway homicides since yesterday and felt the need to catch up.

A live press interview with Eddie Gund was on. Reporters had waylaid him outside his apartment building, demanding a statement concerning the letters he'd written to Chloe LaFleur.

She was thinking he looked like the proverbial stag at bay, when suddenly a stout, middle-aged woman charged out of the building, shouting, "No comment!"

Liz thought the woman looked as if she'd once been on an Olympics track team. In short order she'd rammed through the crowd of newspeople, grabbed hold of Gund's arm, and shepherded him into the building.

Though it had all happened very quickly, Liz got a good enough look at the woman to draw some conclusions. She was too young to be Gund's mother, and since his romantic taste ran to the likes of Chloe LaFleur, her age and general appearance ruled out the chance that she might be a girlfriend.

Was she his sister?

The scene faded. The newscaster returned with comments and information. The woman was, indeed, Gund's twin sister, Edwina, who lived with him.

Twins. Liz's mind teemed with ideas. She'd heard that twins shared a special bond. That could account for the dramatic rescue she'd just witnessed. But could it also be the reason for another kind of rescue—saving her twin brother from a broken heart? Had Eddie Gund's sister known about the glamorous young model and her multiple romances? Had she wanted Chloe out of her brother's life before it was too late?

But, suppose it were true, and twin sister Edwina had killed Chloe LaFleur. The two other victims had no connection to her brother. Why would she have killed them, too?

That question had come full circle again. It applied to every possible suspect. Until it was answered, chances of apprehending the killer would remain slim.

She recalled Sophie's idea of why someone would want to eliminate as many red-haired women as possible. They'd joked about it at the time, but now she put a serious spin on it. What if some tragedy or disaster had happened in the killer's life, for which he held a red-haired woman responsible? What if, over the years, this had gnawed at his mind and twisted it into a psychosis that caused him to blame all red-haired women for his loss or predicament?

That was exactly the train of thought she wanted to avoid, she told herself. She must knock it off before it led her into another wild plan.

Chapter Fourteen

She'd only been at her workstation for a few minutes the next morning, when Ike called.

"I just got word that Valerie Dawes' funeral is at four this afternoon," he said. "I'm going. Any chance you can go with me?"

Ike often went to the funerals of murder victims. He'd told her that observing the people who attended them could sometimes be helpful in solving a case. Recently he'd taken her to one. She welcomed the chance to accompany him to another.

"I'm sure I can work something out with Dan," she replied.

"Good. I'll pick you up at the main entrance at three-thirty."

They entered the Lower East Side funeral home a few minutes before four and found the room where Valerie's service was to take place. A book for callers to enter their names had been placed on a table near the door.

Ike glanced at it, saying, "I don't think it's appropriate for us to sign the book."

Liz nodded in agreement. Their presence here was part of a police investigation.

In the dimly lit room, Valerie's casket stood closed and draped with a blanket of white carnations. As they seated themselves, Liz noticed some vacant chairs.

"I'm surprised it isn't crowded," she whispered. "I thought the news media would be out, full force."

"Under the circumstances, the date and location of the funeral were not made public," Ike replied. "Some reporters might have gotten wind of it, but from the looks of it, not many."

Liz nodded. Valerie's murder had been enough for her family to endure, without her funeral turning into a media circus.

The service began. A young man in a US Army uniform, evidently Valerie's brother, home on leave, opened by reminiscing about Valerie and speaking a few words of eulogy. He was followed by two young women who spoke in turn. Apparently they were close friends of Valerie. Their emotions almost prevented them from getting through what they had to say. After both had stepped down, a man who'd been sitting in the front row of chairs stood up. Liz thought she recognized him from a TV shot.

"Isn't that Dr. Alvin Feldman?" she whispered to Ike.

"Sure is," he whispered back.

The doctor spoke briefly. In a few, moving words, he

stated his deep affection for Valerie. When he sat down, a gentleman, perhaps the family clergyman, Liz thought, led the attendees in prayer, and then it was over.

Liz watched the casket being rolled toward the door by mortuary staff members. Close behind it came the family. After they'd passed by, she noticed Ike studying the crowd following.

Remembering what he'd told her—that sometimes observing people at a murder victim's funeral could be helpful in solving a case—she decided to do the same. As she looked carefully at each passing face, she suddenly caught her breath. She saw a man she recognized instantly. There was no mistaking the squinty eyes of Chloe LaFleur's cameraman, Bernie Weiss!

To get Ike's attention, she clutched his arm, but he must have heard her gasp. He was already looking at her, nodding his head.

"Yeah, I see him," he whispered.

She thought they'd never get out of the building and into Ike's car, where they could talk. There, she wasted no time in expressing her thoughts in questions and comments.

"What was he doing at Valerie's funeral? Surely, it would be too much of a coincidence for him to know *two* of the murder victims! You said that attending the funerals of murder victims could be helpful. Does that mean the killers sometimes show up? Do you think Bernie Weiss could possibly—?"

Ike broke in with a chuckle. "Hold it, Liz. One thing at a time."

"All right. How come he was at the funeral?"

"Good question. I agree with you—there's not much chance of his knowing two of the victims, when they had nothing else in common. It's a long shot, but I suppose he could have come out of curiosity."

Liz shook her head. "How would he know about the funeral? You said it was kept quiet."

"Obviously he heard about it somehow."

"From her brother or her parents?" Liz shook her head. "If he didn't know Valerie, he probably didn't know her family, either. But, however he found out about it, why would he want to attend the funeral of someone with whom he had no connection?"

Ike cast her a grin. "You're building up to saying you think Weiss is the killer."

"Don't you think he could be? Aren't you going to try to find out why he came to the service?"

"Sure. From the moment I saw him there, I decided to pay a call on Valerie's family, tomorrow, and ask them about the people who signed the book."

Liz felt somewhat embarrassed. "That way you'll find out if they know Bernie or not. I should have known you'd be on top of it. I guess I got carried away."

"The circumstances were enough to carry anyone away," he replied.

"Especially someone with my overactive imagination?"

He smiled. "No, anyone at all. By the way, how's your resolution coming along?"

"Pretty well, but it's hard not to lapse back into concentrating too much on the possible suspects and imagining them in wild scenarios."

"I wish the case wasn't keeping me so tied up. Discussing your wild scenarios with me might help."

"Are you going to be tied up tonight?" she asked.

He gave her a rueful look. "Sorry, I am. As soon as I drop you off at your place, I'm meeting Lou at the station house."

She held back a sigh. Another solitary dinner and another evening alone.

While eating a defrosted dinner, she thought about Bernie Weiss. His statement on TV that Chloe had grown too big for her britches meant that their professional relationship had soured. Maybe his experience with Chloe had turned him against all redheads, and his attitude had developed into a psychosis. Maybe he'd decided he had to get rid of her and every other pretty redhead he encountered.

She shook her head. If this were true, wouldn't Chloe have been his first victim? Would he have killed two other redheads before getting around to her?

As usual, her active imagination provided an answer. Maybe one morning Bernie awoke with a plan in his head to kill Chloe. On his way home from work that evening, he bought a hypodermic needle and loaded it with poisonous substances, intending to bring it into his studio the next morning and inject Chloe when she came in for a photo shoot that afternoon. When he boarded the subway and saw red-haired Justine Meister, an uncontrollable urge to kill her came over him.

Then, the next morning, on his way to his studio with another loaded syringe in his pocket, intended for Chloe, he saw red-haired Valerie on the subway platform. Again, the compulsion to kill gripped him.

Chloe's turn didn't come until that evening. By then Bernie would have realized that if he killed her in his studio, he'd have trouble disposing of her body. He'd be the logical one to be charged with her murder, so he waited until she left and followed her to the subway. To avoid having her recognize him in the rush-hour crowd, he probably put on some sort of hat and pulled it down over his face.

Going to the funerals of three women whose lives he had snuffed out would probably give a psychopath some sort of perverted pleasure, but Chloe's service was in Kansas and Justine's was outside of Manhattan. Valerie's was the only one Bernie could attend. She tried to remember the expression on his face in the funeral parlor, but she hadn't gotten beyond recognizing his squinty eyes.

All this seemed to make sense. If only she could run it by Ike. She hoped he didn't have to work again tomorrow night.

Chapter Fifteen

When she awakened the next morning, her thoughts about Bernie Weiss still made sense. Later, when Ike phoned her at work, it was all she could do to keep from telling him what she'd come up with. But it was something that would have to wait until they were together.

"I missed being with you last night," he said. "I'm sorry I've been so tied up lately, but I'll try to make up for it tonight by showing up at your place around six and taking you someplace nice for dinner."

"I like the sound of that. Does it mean the case is going better?"

"Nothing to celebrate yet, but, yeah, there's been a new development. We've gone as far as we could on it for now, so I'm all yours for the evening."

Could the new development have anything to do with Bernie Weiss? She wondered. "Can you tell me about the new development tonight?" she asked.

"I promise to give you all the details."

"Good. I'll see you around six."

"Dinner someplace nice," Ike had said. That meant *wearing* something nice.

When she got home, she went through her clothes closet to make a selection. She had several dressy outfits she'd worn only a couple of times. They were left over from what she called her pre-Ike days, when a dinner date meant going out to one of Manhattan's poshest places. Once Ike got serious about her, those guys were history, and posh-place eating had mostly given way to takeout, but her clothes were still in style.

She chose a knee-length, black, A-line skirt and a long-sleeved, black, silk-knit sweater with chiffon ruffling around the V-neckline. A turquoise necklace fit perfectly within the neckline. Black high-heeled pumps and a black wool jacket completed the outfit.

When Ike arrived, he told her he'd made dinner reservations at a restaurant on the Battery. "I've never been there, but I hear the food is great and it overlooks the harbor," he said. "I asked for a table where we'll have a view of the water and the Statue of Liberty." He cast her a grin, adding, "Very romantic."

Also very expensive, Liz thought. Ike must be trying to compensate for their many take-out dinners, the eat-and-runs, and the evenings, past and future, that he couldn't spend with her.

When they arrived at the restaurant, she was pleased with the ambience, and when they were shown to their table, she was delighted. "You were right—this *is* romantic," she said, gazing through a window at the dark water sparked with reflections of lights from passing boats, and accentuated by a magnificent view of a radiant Lady Liberty.

They ordered glasses of Chablis and skewers of shrimp with a zesty sauce, followed by fresh salmon steaks with onion marmalade and couscous, and a crisp, crunchy salad. For dessert, chocolate mousse topped by whipped cream and silvered almonds made Liz sigh in contentment.

"Beats takeout, doesn't it?" Ike asked.

"Yes, but I'd rather eat takeout with you than a meal like this with anyone else," she replied.

He smiled. "Remarks like that could charm the hardest heart," he said. "How come the Irish are so good at blarney?"

"I wasn't so good at it with Aunt Hilda," she said.

"Oh!" he exclaimed with a shake of his head. "Where's my mind tonight? I forgot to tell you my folks phoned this afternoon, and wait till you hear this. Aunt Hilda's keeping them in her will! She's still standing firm about me and our wedding, but you managed to turn her around as far as my folks are concerned."

Liz stared at him in utter disbelief.

"It's true," Ike said. "She called Dad at his office this morning and told him."

That new development in the case must be on his mind, Liz thought. It must be important to cause him to forget something so momentous. Again she thought of

Bernie Weiss but told herself it was too soon for him to have found out anything in that area. Whatever the new development was, he'd promised to let her in on it tonight. Meanwhile, his announcement about Aunt Hilda made her very happy.

"I guess I don't have to tell you, I'm ecstatic about your great-aunt's change of heart," she said.

He nodded. "I know you were feeling that her cutting Mother and Dad out of her will was your fault. That's all over now."

He paid the bill. They took one last look at the view before leaving the table.

"Thanks for a very special evening," she said, as they made their way toward the entrance. "And the news about Aunt Hilda topped it off like icing on a delicious cake."

Suddenly, she did a double take. Even in the restaurant's dim light, the burnished copper color of Paula Rubik's flowing hair was an eye-catcher. She was sitting a couple of aisles away, engrossed in talk with a young man, dark-haired and extremely handsome.

"There's one of Dr. Jurgens' assistants, the woman I told you about," Liz said. "I can't believe she's still going around bareheaded with all that red hair."

Ike took a look. "I recall seeing her when I was there. She looks different with her hair loose like that. She had it tied back while she was working."

He continued to look for a few moments. "I hope you don't want to stop to speak to her," he said.

The tone of his voice and the expression on his face suggested he wanted to get back to her apartment without delay, Liz thought. Well, so did she. She was itching to hear what he had to tell her—and to tell him her own ideas about Bernie Weiss.

She shook her head. "Oh, no, I want to go home and hear about the new development in the subway murders. Besides, she and her boyfriend look as if they don't want to be disturbed."

Ike made no comment until they'd left the restaurant. As soon as they were outside, he said, "That guy's no boyfriend."

She looked at him in surprise. "What makes you think he isn't?"

"Because I know who he is—or, I should say, *what* he is. He gets paid for taking women out on the town. He works for an escort service."

Chapter Sixteen

Liz stared at Ike. "Are you sure you're not mistaken?" she asked. "An attractive woman like Paula wouldn't have to pay someone to take her places."

"There's no mistake."

His blunt reply made Liz think he'd encountered Paula's dinner companion in connection with a case. It also suggested that whatever had happened, the man had not been a witness or an innocent bystander.

"This is hard for me to believe," she said. "Maybe Paula doesn't know what he does for a living."

"That's possible, of course," he replied.

"She could have met him somewhere," Liz continued. "Maybe they use the same dry cleaner or something and kept running into each other, and then . . ."

"Or maybe they met in church," Ike growled.

Liz ignored the sarcasm. "If he really likes her, do you think he'd want to come clean with her and tell her

143

the truth about himself?" *Including what had gotten him involved with the NYPD?* Ike had been closemouthed about that. Curious as she was, she felt reluctant to press for details.

"I wouldn't count on his being honest with her about his job or anything else," Ike replied.

When they were in the car, Liz gave the matter some more thought. Whether or not Paula knew her dinner companion was an escort-for-hire, it seemed unlikely that he'd tell her about his brush with the law. Suppose she was seeing him regularly, and the offense had been serious. Paula might be in danger.

"*Someone* should tell her," she said.

Ike gave a groan. "I hope you're not thinking of telling her yourself. I'm not issuing orders, but I'd like you to stay out of it."

Worrying about her getting involved in the matter was the last thing Ike needed, Liz thought. She knew she must scrap any ideas she had of letting Paula know the truth.

"All right," she said. "I promise I won't say a word to her about it. Maybe I won't see her again, anyway. She mentioned getting together some Sunday for a movie, but that might have been just talk, like, 'Let's do lunch.'"

He gave her hand a squeeze. "Good."

At that moment, she considered asking him if Paula's companion had committed a felony. She backed off. If she and Paula *did* get together sometime, she'd feel uncomfortable with this information. It would be awkward enough knowing he was an escort for hire.

* * *

In her apartment, Liz made coffee. She and Ike took their mugs to the sofa and settled themselves among Gram's needlepoint pillows.

After some snuggling and talk about their forthcoming wedding, Ike looked at her with a quizzical smile.

"You're really sticking to your resolution," he said. "I thought by now you'd be hounding me about the new development in the case."

"I was just about to start hounding." She looked at him expectantly.

"Okay, here goes. Several people have come forward in response to NYPD messages on radio and TV," he said. "We didn't expect more than one or two. Generally, people are reluctant to admit they were anywhere near the scene of a homicide. Up until now, the only witnesses we had were the ones who helped the victims or called 911."

One or more of the people who'd come forward must have provided new information, or Ike wouldn't consider this important, Liz thought.

"Of those who responded, two were on the evening rush-hour train when Justine was helped off," Ike continued. "One was on the subway platform the next morning and saw Valerie collapse, and three saw Chloe faint on a subway car during rush hour that night."

"Did they come up with anything helpful?" Liz asked.

"Yeah, the information's still restricted, but . . ." His smile told her he was going to waive the restriction for her. "The man and woman who witnessed Justine's being helped off said they noticed a man crowded close to her in the packed car," Ike continued. "They said he got off at the next station, and after the train started moving again, the girl seemed to be feeling faint. They saw a woman help her off the train at the next stop."

"With all the men in that crowded car, how could they have noticed any particular one?" Liz asked.

"He had on a brown felt hat with a wide brim pulled down over his eyes."

"A fedora?"

"Right."

"Did any of the others notice this guy?"

"Yeah. One of the men was on the subway platform during morning rush hour, waiting for a train, when he noticed a pretty, red-haired girl. A few minutes later, while he was boarding the train, he saw her keel over on the platform."

"That was Valerie, on her way to work."

"Right. And he said he'd seen a man wearing a wide-brimmed fedora standing close to her in the crowd, but the man didn't get on the train. The same thing happened with Chloe. Two men reported seeing a beautiful, red-haired woman in the crowd waiting for a train. She boarded the same car as they did, and a few minutes later they saw her faint. Both of them said they'd noticed a man wearing a brown felt hat with a very wide brim standing next to her on the platform. Both were certain he didn't get on the train."

"He jabbed and ran," Liz said. "Did any of the witnesses describe him?"

"Briefly. They didn't get far beyond the wide-brimmed fedora, but most of them said he had swarthy skin and seemed young, maybe in his late twenties or early thirties, and three of them said he had a mustache."

Liz pondered this. All the witnesses had noticed the wide-brimmed fedora. If someone were planning a murder in the subway, why would he risk calling attention to himself by wearing something so easily identified? Liz wondered. A moment later she thought she might have the answer.

Ike's voice broke into her thoughts. "That steel-trap mind of yours has latched on to something, hasn't it?"

"Thanks for the kind words about my mind, but after you hear what I've been thinking, you might want to rephrase," she replied. "Maybe it's just my imagination going out of control again."

He drew her into a hug. "Don't knock your imagination. It's part of your ability to figure things out. I've said it before, and I'll say it again—you'd make one hell of a detective, Redlocks. What have you come up with now?"

She told him what she'd been thinking about Bernie Weiss. "And now that you've told me about the wide-brimmed felt hat, I feel as if there might be a connection." She paused, adding, "You must have noticed Bernie's eyes."

"Yeah, they're very squinty." Suddenly, he pulled her into a hug.

"I get it, Redlocks. That wide-brimmed hat would hide his eyes and help keep him from being identified."

"You don't think it's a crazy idea?"

"A bit far out, maybe, but in homicides, anything goes. This might tie in with the new information we're working on."

The information given by the witnesses had boosted Ike's spirits, and her thoughts about Bernie Weiss had added to it, Liz thought. "I can tell you're encouraged," she said.

He nodded. "I am. Now we have something tangible to work on."

"Are you going to search Bernie's apartment for the hat?"

"Not yet. First I need to go to Valerie's parents' home and question them about the people who signed the funeral-parlor book. If they draw a blank on Bernie, we'll take it from there."

At last she felt as if she might have helped him!

Later, when he said he should be going, he told her he hoped the news media would not get hold of the wide-brimmed hat angle right away. "If the guy in the over-sized fedora is the killer, he'd quit wearing it, and we'd miss our chance to nab him," he said, as they walked to the door. He paused, looking into her eyes with a smile. "Unless, of course, we find out that nobody in Valerie's family ever heard of Bernie Weiss, and a hat like that turns up in his apartment."

She returned the smile, loving him for never putting down her ideas.

"Thanks for a beautiful evening," she said, kissing him. "Besides the delicious food, the setting was wonderful, too. With the view of the harbor lights and the Statue of Liberty, it was . . ."

"Romantic?" he asked with a grin.

"Very," she replied.

"We haven't had enough of that lately," he said.

"We'll go there again whcn I have another free evening. Let's hope next time your red-haired friend and her escort aren't there." He paused. "I know what I told you about him upset you. Maybe I should have kept my mouth shut."

She told him she was okay with it. "It's not as if she's really a friend," she said. "But I'd be concerned about anyone I thought might be setting herself up for danger."

The kissed good-night. He said he'd be working late the next day, but he'd call her.

Despite her brimming mind, Liz had no trouble falling asleep, and the thoughts that crowded her head evolved into a bizarre dream. When she awakened in the morning, parts of it still lingered. While showering and dressing, she reviewed what she could remember of it.

Gram and her kitten and everyone on Ike's list of possible suspects, including Bernie Weiss, were in her apartment. She'd invited them all for dinner but realized she hadn't cooked anything. She was wondering what to do, when Paula Rubik arrived, followed by Aunt Hilda and Ike, who was carrying an armload of Chinese takeout.

Clearly the result of an overcrowded mind, she told herself while brewing coffee and toasting a bagel.

On her way to work, she thought about the dream. She must remember to tell Ike about it. He'd get a laugh out of it, especially the part about his coming in with Aunt Hilda and the Chinese takeout.

Chapter Seventeen

The next morning, while walking to the crosstown bus, Liz phoned Gram to tell her about the disastrous visit with Aunt Hilda and its happy outcome.

Gram hung on every word. "I can't believe there are still people around who think that way," she said. "It's been almost fifty years since Pope John—God bless his soul—did away with many of the rules that separated Catholics from other religions."

"Pope John came along too late for Aunt Hilda," Liz replied.

"But you came along in time for her to change her mind about cutting Ike's folks out of her will," Gram said. "Too bad she's still stubborn about your wedding, but at least you accomplished most of what you set out to do."

After inquiring about Hercules and being told he was developing into a wonderful pet, Liz reached the bus stop and sighted the bus approaching. Still listening to Gram's praises about the kitten, she got in line to board.

"When are you getting together with your new friend?" Gram asked suddenly.

"New friend?" Liz asked in puzzlement.

"You know—that rich girl, Paula, at the veterinarian's," Gram said.

"Oh . . . Paula . . . I don't know. She said she'd call me."

"You sound as if you don't care whether or not she does. I thought you liked her."

"I do, and I thought she'd be good company for me when Ike's tied up working."

"Oh, there's someone at my door," Gram said. "I have to hang up. Have a good day, dear."

A few minutes after Liz arrived at work, Sophie phoned from her patrol car. "Word around the station house has the detectives putting in big overtime on the subway homicides," she said. "Did you get to see Ike last night?"

"Yes, we spent the whole evening together. We had dinner at the most romantic place. It's on the Battery, with a great view of the harbor and the Statue of . . ." Her voice trailed off. In her mind's eye she saw Paula and the hired escort, deep in conversation.

Sophie must have thought they'd lost their connection. "Liz? Are you there?" she asked.

"Yes, I'm here. Can you talk for a few more minutes?"

"Sure. Mike just went into a doughnut shop to get us coffee. What's up?"

"It's about that woman I told you about, the one who works for the veterinarian."

"Ms. Moneybags? What about her?"

Liz told her about seeing Paula in the restaurant. "But she didn't see me. She was absorbed in talk with a very good-looking man. I assumed he was her boyfriend, but after I pointed them out to Ike, he told me the guy works for an escort service."

"How would Ike know he—?" Abruptly, Sophie cut off her question. "Uh-oh," she said. "Ike remembered busting him! Did he say what for?"

"He didn't go into details, and I don't want to know."

"I get it, "Sophie replied. "It's bad enough knowing she was out on the town with a gigolo—but a gigolo maybe with a rap sheet for God knows what? I agree, you're better off not knowing why he was collared."

"And Paula would be better off in the dark about what Ike told me. I promised him I wouldn't mention any of this to her if I saw her again."

"You sound as if you're not sure about seeing her again. I thought you wanted something to do while Ike's tied up on the case."

"I still do, and I'll take in a movie or dinner with Paula if she contacts me when I'm at loose ends."

"Well, I gotta go," Sophie said. "Let me know if you get together with Ms. Moneybags and if you find out anything about her and the gigolo."

Soon after she and Sophie said good-bye, Ike phoned

to remind her he'd be working most of the evening. "Dinner's out," he said, "But I'll call you to let you know if I can make it later on."

Home from work, Liz decided to microwave one of the frozen entrées she kept on hand for the evenings when Ike couldn't make it for dinner. Fortunately, those evenings were few and far between. She missed not eating with him.

She took a box of spaghetti and meatballs out of the freezer, thinking it was a good thing Rosa couldn't see her. For Rosa, Italian dishes were not worth eating unless they were made from recipes handed down from an Old Country great-grandmother, and the area around the stove looked like the scene of a massacre.

Before she put the frozen entree into the microwave, the phone rang. *Ike, calling to say he could make it for dinner after all!* Smiling in anticipation, she threw the box back into the freezer and grabbed the phone.

"Hello?"

"Hello, Liz, this is Paula Rubik."

"Oh, hi." Liz hoped her disappointment wasn't too obvious.

"I called to see if you're free next Sunday afternoon for a movie," Paula said.

Suddenly, the prospect of tonight's solitary micro-waved dinner caught up with Liz. "I don't know about Sunday yet, Paula, but if you're free for dinner tonight, so am I. Maybe we could meet at a restaurant."

She'd spoken on impulse, and a moment later she

wished she hadn't. Paula had money to burn. She might suggest meeting in some ultraupscale place where the entrées cost more than a week's groceries.

"Yes, I'm free for dinner," Paula replied, sounding pleased. "But if you don't mind, I'd rather not eat at a restaurant tonight. We're having a very busy day, and I know that by quitting time I'll feel like taking off my shoes and relaxing. How about having dinner at my apartment? We'll order in from a wonderful little catering place I discovered in my neighborhood."

A *pricey* little catering place, Liz guessed. "Dinner at your apartment sounds good," she said. "But don't bother ordering from the caterer. I can stop on my way and get takeout."

She imagined Paula shaking her head. "The food from the catering place will be so much better. Of course it will cost more, but don't worry—it will be my treat."

It was as if she were saying, *"I'm rich, and you're not."*

Thanks," Liz replied. "What time?"

"I'm still at work, but I'm leaving shortly. "Here's my address. . . ."

"That's not too far from where I live," Liz said. "I could walk it in about fifteen minutes."

"Take a cab," Paula said. "The area's safe, even after dark, but you never know."

"All right, I'll take a cab," Liz said. "See you later—about six-thirty or so?"

"Fine," Paula replied. "I'll tell the doorman I'm expecting you."

Right after they hung up, Liz decided to call Sophie and tell her about the dinner with Paula. She called Sophie's cell phone number. Whether Sophie was still on the job or in her apartment, she'd get the call.

Sophie picked up right away. "Liz? Hi."

"Where are you? Can you talk?"

"Sure, I'm on my way home. What's up?"

"I just wanted to tell you I'm having dinner with Ms. Moneybags tonight at her place. I'll try to find out more about the paid escort."

"Good. Did you tell Ike you're going there for dinner?"

"No. I talked with him earlier, before I set this up with Paula. He said he'd be working late and he'd call again to tell me if he'd be over later. I don't like to phone him when he's on the job. I hope he calls before I leave for Paula's; otherwise, he'll be wondering where I am."

"Ike could be trying to reach you now, so we shouldn't tie up the line," Sophie said.

When Ike didn't phone by the time she was ready to go, Liz decided that he must be extremely busy. She'd probably be home from Paula's before he got around to calling. Meanwhile, dinner with Paula would fill up an otherwise-lonely evening.

Chapter Eighteen

The taxi driver pulled up at a building with an awning extending from its well-lighted entrance to the curb. Liz had just paid the fare when a uniformed doorman appeared, hurrying between huge containers of evergreen shrubs flanking the walkway.

"Good evening, miss," he said, opening the cab door. "Are you the lady Miss Rubik is expecting?"

"Yes," Liz replied. Paula wasn't exaggerating when she said this was a posh apartment.

The doorman led the way to a glass double door embellished with gleaming brass. In the lobby, he ushered her across an expanse of marble flooring into a waiting elevator and pressed a button. "Miss Rubik's apartment is on the third floor," he said. As he left, he took a phone off his belt, saying, "I'll notify her you're on your way up."

This place was as secure as Fort Knox, Liz thought. She recalled Paula's saying she'd gotten a pedigreed

Doberman as a guard dog. She certainly didn't need one here.

When the elevator door slid open, Paula was in the corridor, waiting. She must have changed clothes when she'd gotten home from work, Liz thought. She had on lime green palazzo pants topped by a jungle-print tunic. Her hair looked even brighter than Liz remembered. *Gram had it right. That color had come out of a bottle, and it looked as if it had just been enhanced.*

"Hi, Liz. It's good to see you. I'm so pleased you were free," she said.

When Paula opened the door of her apartment, Liz had to hold back a gasp. Although she'd expected it to reflect the Rubik-Rockefeller affluence, the sheer opulence of obviously expensive modern furnishings, blended with what looked like priceless antiques, almost overwhelmed her. She'd never seen anything to equal it, even on TV or in home-decorating magazines.

"Your apartment is beautiful, Paula," she managed to say.

"Thanks. I had it professionally decorated. Cost me a mint." Paula gestured toward a luxurious-looking couch and a glass-topped table with a tray of crystal goblets and a decanter. "Let's have a glass of wine while we're waiting for dinner to be delivered. I ordered broiled lobster and a linguine-and-artichoke salad with black olives and almonds, and their little Italian pastries for dessert. I hope that's okay with you."

"It sounds wonderful," Liz replied. *Like she'd rather have pizza?*

"I didn't order coffee," Paula said. "I keep a special,

very expensive after-dinner blend on hand, if you're not anti-caffeine."

Liz shook her head. "No, I enjoy a good cup of coffee after dinner."

Especially when Ike was there, enjoying it with her, she thought. Had he phoned her apartment yet? Suddenly, she realized she'd forgotten to bring her cell phone with her. Well, chances were he was so tied up on the case tonight that she'd get home before he was free to call her.

How was the investigation going? She recalled that, before she left her apartment, she hadn't turned on her TV to catch this evening's news. Something could have happened.

"Paula, do you mind if I check out the news on TV to see if anything has developed on the subway murders?" she asked. As she spoke, she looked around the room for a television screen. She didn't see one, but in a place like this it would probably be concealed in an antique chest or something, she thought.

"I haven't heard any news about that all day either. I'd like an update, too," Paula replied, picking up a remote-control device from a nearby table. An instant later two wall panels opposite the couch slid away, revealing the largest TV screen Liz had ever seen.

A news channel came on. Liz felt a pang of disappointment when she found herself viewing a rerun of Eddie Gund's twin sister rescuing him from reporters. "Looks like there's nothing new," she said.

"There hasn't been anything new for days," Paula

replied. "But let's keep the TV on mute, on the chance something develops."

She turned to the wine tray and picked up the decanter. One whiff of the pale golden liquid in her goblet told Liz this was no supermarket four-pack wine. Like everything else in this lavishly appointed apartment, it was top-notch. Including the pedigreed Doberman pinscher. Where was he? She hadn't heard any barking when they entered the apartment.

"Is your dog here, Paula?" she asked.

"Brutus is back in the storeroom," Paula replied. "He's such a barker. I didn't want him sounding off when we came in, and again when our dinner's delivered." She gave a sigh. "The building owner lives in the apartment next door, and he's been complaining. It costs tenants an extra hundred dollars a month to have pets here. You'd think he could put up with a little barking."

The bark of a full-grown Doberman could hardly be described as "little," Liz thought.

Paula curled up on the couch with her goblet and took a generous drink. "Speaking of pets, how's your grandmother getting along with the kitten?" she asked.

"Great," Liz replied. "She's very happy with him."

"Next time you talk to her, give her my best." Paula quaffed a bit more wine. "It's funny how things happen," she said. "If you hadn't been looking for a kitten for your grandmother to adopt, we probably never would have met, but here we are, getting to be friends. It isn't easy to make friends in New York, but I knew I liked you the minute we started talking that night outside

Dr. Jurgens' office. I knew you were a caring person when you told me you were concerned about my taking the subway with my hair uncovered. I'm glad we found each other, Liz."

The commendation embarrassed Liz. Paula was okay, but she couldn't make a similar statement in return. Instead, she did the best she could.

"Even after you told me you never ride the subway, I was concerned about your hair," she replied. She took a small drink from her goblet, adding, "I still am. There've been no more redheads murdered in the subway since the weather turned cold, but the killer could change his MO."

Paula looked puzzled. "MO—what's that?"

Liz laughed. "I guess you don't watch *Law & Order* or the other cop shows on TV. MO is short for *modus operandi,* or *method of operation.*"

Paula nodded. "You're right—I'm not a cop show fan." She paused, as if pondering. "So you think maybe the killer will start killing redheads again in a different way and a different area?"

"It's possible."

"What can I do?" Paula asked, looking troubled. "My hair's too long to hide under a scarf or hat, and I don't want to cut it."

Liz was about to tell her she'd dyed her red hair brown and to suggest that Paula also make a color change, when Paula suddenly brightened. "I know! I'll get a skullcap. It will hold my hair secure under a scarf or hat."

"Good idea, but skullcaps aren't exactly common merchandise," Liz replied. "Where are you going to find one?"

"I don't know. Do you think a theatrical costume rental place would have one?"

"Right—in a place like that, you're sure to find exactly what you're looking for."

"I don't want the only friend I've found in New York to lose any sleep over me," Paula said with a smile. She drank some more wine and leaned back on the couch, saying, "As I said before, making friends in New York isn't easy. When I first came here and moved into this building, I thought I was lucky when I met a good-looking man whose apartment was just across the hall. We started seeing each other."

So Paula had a boyfriend, Liz thought. "What do you mean you *thought* you were lucky?" she asked. "Sounds like a stroke of luck to me."

Paula shook her head. Her face saddened. "It didn't last. His company transferred him to the West Coast, and I never heard from him again."

It sounded as if Paula might have fallen in love with this guy, Liz thought. "How long has he been gone?" she asked, thinking perhaps he'd get in touch with her when he got settled.

"More than two months," Paula replied. "There hasn't been anyone else since. And until you came along, I haven't made any women friends, either." Her voice choked as she added, "I've been very lonesome, especially now that we're going into the Christmas season."

At that moment, her doorbell sounded.

"That's our dinner," Paula said, brushing at her eyes and getting up from the couch. She managed a wan smile. "Just in time to keep me from crying into my wine."

Liz was thankful for the interruption. The emotional confidence left her feeling uncomfortable.

They took the caterer's bags into a kitchen resplendent with tile, stainless steel, and granite, and set up the food on a round table near a window. Paula brought their wine goblets and the decanter from the living room. "Don't worry, I'm not going to stage another crying jag," she said. "Those lobsters look too scrumptious for me to stay depressed."

The meal was a gourmet delight. By the time they were finished and settled in the living room with coffee, Paula had put away two more goblets of wine, but, true to her statement, she steered clear of any talk about being lonesome. Instead, while glancing at the TV to make sure she didn't miss a bulletin about the subway homicides, Liz listened to a monologue about Paula's life. Her family was oil rich. She grew up on a ranch. She had no close living relatives. "Only some cousins back in Oklahoma," Paula said.

"You're so fond of animals, and you had all kinds of pets, including horses," Liz said. "Don't you miss that?"

"It was great when I was a kid, but we lived near what can only be described as a one-mule town. Going to the university gave me a taste of what life could be away from the sticks, but it wasn't enough. I'd heard about New York City on TV and read about it in magazines. I wanted to go to the famous museums and art galleries and the opera. I wanted to see Broadway shows and take in New York's nightlife, but most of all, I wanted to meet a cultured, sophisticated man who'd show me around town, and who . . ." She paused, shaking her head. "For a while I thought I'd found him. I thought I had it all."

This was getting dangerously close to the lonesome talk, Liz thought. She didn't want to go through that again. Just as she was wondering how to divert it, something else struck her. Ever since the man across the hall moved across the country, Paula had been not only lonesome—she also missed going out to all the exciting, glamorous places he'd taken her. To fill the void, she had turned to an escort service. *Did she have the same hired escort each time?*

Liz hoped not. Going out regularly with a man who had a police record was asking for trouble. After a few dates with this guy, Paula might grow to trust him. She might think it was okay to have him come to her apartment instead of meeting him in the lobby. Paula was no dumbbell, but in her lonely state she might be vulnerable. What if this guy was a con artist? Or a jewel thief? Or a sexual predator?

Liz held back a deep sigh. One of the plaguing thoughts on her mind had gone away when Paula said she'd hide her hair under a skullcap. The other seemed to have magnified.

She'd promised Ike she wouldn't say one word to Paula about seeing her in the restaurant with a handsome man. *How could she find out if Paula hired that same escort every time?*

Paula's voice, slightly slurred, continued her monologue. "It was wonderful while it lasted. I was sure all my dreams were coming true. And then he was gone." She stared into her empty goblet.

Liz didn't know what to say, but it didn't matter. Paula was already talking again.

"It's been good confiding in you, Liz. I know I've monopolized our conversation, talking about myself. I didn't give you a chance to tell me anything about yourself and your family. . . ." She glanced at Liz's engagement ring. Her face saddened. "And of course your fiancé."

Liz felt a rush of sympathy. The old adage that money does not buy happiness was certainly true where Paula was concerned.

"If I tell you something else, will you promise not to be shocked?" Paula asked.

"Sure . . ." Liz had a sudden inkling of what was coming. She was right.

Paula didn't mince words. "I've been going out with men who get paid for being escorts," she blurted.

Liz grabbed on to her use of the plural. That sounded as if Paula didn't go out with the same escort every time.

"So you've dated a few guys who work for an escort service," she said, putting on a careless shrug.

Paula gave her a grateful smile. "I should have known you wouldn't disapprove. I'm not proud of it, but I look at it this way. I'm a lonely woman who wants to go out once in a while to dinner or the theatre or a nightclub, and those men are providing a needed service."

How many times had she gone out with the guy Ike had recognized? Liz wondered. "I'm curious," she said. "When you call in for an escort, can you request a previous one you liked, or do you have to take what comes?"

"You can ask for a certain one. I've done that several times. There's one man who's especially smooth and good-looking and knows his way around town."

Was that the man Ike had recognized? Liz wondered. Whether or not he was, at least one of her concerns about Paula was ended. If the subway killer changed his MO and went looking for redheaded victims in some crowded place where Paula might be, her hair would be bundled under a skullcap and a scarf or hat.

Suddenly she'd had enough of this. She wanted to go home and wait for Ike.

"I should be leaving soon," she said.

Paula nodded. "Before you go, I want to introduce you to Brutus. Then, every time you come here, he'll remember you, and I won't have to shut him in the storeroom to keep him from barking."

Every time you come here! Paula was assuming she'd found a real pal in New York, and from now on they'd be having dinner together frequently either here or in some expensive restaurant, Liz thought. She liked Paula and felt sorry she was lonely, but tonight had made her realize how far out of Paula's league she was, financially. Having dinner regularly with the Rubik heiress would really flatten the Rooney wallet. An occasional get-together when Ike was working would be all right, but that was it.

They walked down a short corridor to a door, where Paula took a key off a hook above it. "If I don't lock the door, Brutus knows how to wiggle the knob until the door springs open," she said, turning the key. "He's very smart."

Also very big, Liz thought, eyeing the Doberman.

Eyeing her in return, Brutus let out a volley of thunderous barks before Paula convinced him Liz was no threat.

"This has been a great evening," Paula said. "Next time, I promise I'll let *you* do some talking."

At the door, she picked up the intercom. "I'll call Lamar, the doorman, and ask him to hail a cab for you," she said. "That way it will be waiting for you by the time you get to the lobby."

Liz stepped off the elevator, walked through the lobby, and left the building. The doorman was standing outside, but there was no cab there. When he saw her, he hastened to explain.

"Miss Rubik called down about getting you a taxi, miss," he said.

Liz noticed he was looking at her strangely, as if he were puzzled or curious. "But I didn't have to," he continued. "A . . . a gentleman came looking for you a little while ago."

Gesturing toward a No Parking zone near the entrance, he added, "He said not to bother calling Miss Rubik's apartment. He showed me a police badge and said he'd park his car over there and wait till you came down."

Chapter Nineteen

Ike! He was out of the Taurus and striding toward her. She flashed the doorman a quick smile, waved at Ike, and hurried to meet him.

"I'm sure the doorman expects you to take me away in handcuffs," she said, when they were face-to-face.

"This should set him straight," Ike replied, sweeping her into his arms and planting a sizeable kiss on her mouth. "I hope you don't mind my tracking you down like this. I wanted to see you as soon as I could."

"It was a pleasant surprise," she replied. "But how did you know where I was?"

"When I couldn't get you by phone, I thought you might be over at Sophie and Ralph's, so I called them, and Sophie said you were having dinner with Paula Rubik. I looked up her address in the phone book."

"But how did you know we weren't eating out somewhere?" Liz asked as they got into the Taurus.

"I questioned the doorman. He told me Miss Rubik had had dinner sent in, and she and her guest hadn't left the building," Ike replied, maneuvering the car into the traffic. "I didn't want to go up to her apartment and butt into your visit. I told the doorman I'd wait for you down here."

Liz laughed. "In a No Parking area? Shame on you, flashing your badge for a nonessential matter."

"The end justified the means," he replied with a grin.

"Too bad you didn't get to see Paula's apartment. The furnishings are absolutely fabulous! You wouldn't believe the size of the TV screen."

"Anyone who can take cabs everywhere and lives in that building and hires paid escorts wouldn't have a thirteen-inch TV," Ike replied.

"Oh, by the way, I don't have to worry anymore about Paula's hair," Liz said.

"Yeah? Did you tell her you're a redhead and you dyed your hair, and she decided to do it, too?"

Liz laughed. "No. I didn't get a chance to tell her anything about myself. Paula talked about Paula the entire time, except when I managed to get in a few words about the subway killer's possibly changing his MO. That shook her up, and she agreed to do something about her hair. She said it was too long to hide under a scarf or a hat, and then she came up with the idea of a skullcap."

"A skullcap?" Ike paused, as if giving this some serious thought. "Yeah," he said with a nod. "She could pack that mane of hers into it and wear whatever she wanted over it, even a wig."

"At least *that's* off my mind," Liz said.

Braking the Taurus at a stoplight, Ike cast her a quizzical look. "Did she say anything about that guy from the escort service?"

"Yes." She told him about Paula's repeated dates with a man she favored. "If this one is the man you busted, she could be headed for trouble. You asked me not to warn her, and of course I didn't, but can't you let me know what he was charged with? If it's nothing serious, I'll forget about it."

Ike was silent for a moment as he accelerated the car on the green light. "Okay," he said. "He was booked on suspicion of bilking an elderly woman out of her nest egg, but the charges didn't stick."

"Do you believe he was guilty?"

He nodded. "But if you're imagining this guy taking Paula for all she's worth, I think you can forget it. From what you told me about her, she's a lightweight in some ways, but she's not some naïve little old lady, and she's not a gullible young girl, either. She sounds like she's too savvy to be duped by a con artist."

Ike had pegged Paula pretty well, Liz thought. "You're right—she wouldn't be an easy mark," she replied.

An idea flashed into her mind. "Besides," she said, "Paula's money comes from family wealth. Wouldn't there be estate attorneys looking after it?"

"Yeah, I should think so. Most of her cash would be safe. Let's hope she doesn't flaunt valuable jewelry when she goes out with this guy."

"Well, we've talked enough about Paula," Liz said. "Anything new on the case?"

"Yeah, we found out that Mrs. Sinclair was seeing a shrink for a while."

Right away, Liz remembered her previous speculation about Mrs. Sinclair's mental state.

"Ooh. Were you able to get any details?"

"No. Doctor-patient confidentiality's almost impossible to breach—but finding out she was a psychiatric patient is a lead. We hope to pick up details from other sources."

Such as friends, acquaintances, even members or former members of the Sinclair household staff, Liz thought. They might have noticed mood swings, odd behavior, or something. Suddenly, she recalled Sophie's idea about someone developing a hatred for redheads and deciding to kill as many of them as he could.

"Of course, seeing a shrink doesn't mean a person is a psychopath," Ike was saying. "And just because someone has never been under psychiatric care doesn't mean he or she is *not* one. Seeing psychiatrists has become commonplace in recent years."

"I know, but I just thought of something," Liz said.

They'd reached the Moscarettis' brownstone. Ike pulled the Taurus into a space and braked. "About Mrs. Sinclair?" he asked.

"Well, not directly. It's based on an idea Sophie had."

"Let's hear it."

Whatever he might think of this, she needed to run it by him. "Okay," she said. "Is there any way you could find out if the Sinclairs ever employed a red-haired nanny?"

He looked at her in puzzlement. "Why?"

"I got to thinking that if Giles had been abused by a red-haired nanny when he was a little kid, his mother might have developed an intense dislike of all red-heads."

She thought he might laugh at the idea. Instead, he gave her a hug, saying, "And you think because she's been seeing a shrink, she might be mentally off-balance enough kill the redhead she thought her son might be in love with? Interesting concept, Redlocks. I'll look into it."

"So you think my idea makes some sense?" she asked.

"Sure, it does. If it turns out that Giles had a red-haired nanny, we'd be two steps ahead. We'd have vital information to back up anything we might get from the psychiatrist or other sources. Not only that, but it might provide an explanation for the murder of the two other redheads."

"What if there was never a red-haired nanny?"

"Nothing ventured, nothing gained." He gave her another hug, along with a kiss. "After all the helpful ideas you've come up with in past cases, I know by now not to take any one of them lightly," he said.

She remembered he hadn't taken lightly her idea about Bernie Weiss' wearing a wide-brimmed hat to hide his squinty eyes.

"Have you found out anything more about the man in the fedora?" she asked.

"No, but we found out why Bernie Weiss came to Valerie's funeral. He wasn't there for some perverse reason. He and Dr. Alvin Feldman have been close friends for years. They were in school together."

He must have seen the disappointed look in her eyes.

He gave her hand a pat. "But that doesn't rule him out as the fedora man."

"No, but it makes him seem like a nice, sympathetic person," Liz replied. "Besides, if he and the doctor are such close buddies, wouldn't he know Valerie? Would he kill the girlfriend of his childhood pal just because she was a redhead?"

"There's no telling what a psychopath would do," Ike replied.

They went up the steps of the brownstone.

"Looks like the Moscarettis have hit the sack early," Ike said, eyeing the dark front window.

Liz nodded her approval. That meant Rosa wouldn't pop out of her apartment, as she often did, and invite them in for a snack. Much as she loved Rosa and Joe, she wanted to be alone with Ike for the rest of the evening.

"Are you hungry?" she asked, as they climbed the stairs to her apartment. "I could fix something for you."

"Thanks, but we grabbed hamburgers at a fast-food place," he replied. "I could use some coffee, though."

Behind the screen that concealed what passed for a kitchen, she started the coffeemaker, and Ike took two mugs out of the lone cabinet. In contrast to this cramped, makeshift cooking space, thoughts of Paula's state-of-the-art kitchen crowded her mind: the sink that resembled a Roman fountain, the stove with a panel of knobs and dials that looked like the cockpit of a jetliner, the invisible refrigerator, the temperature-controlled wine rack. Paula's kitchen had everything in it except a man like Ike, she thought. She wouldn't trade kitchens with Paula for all the money in the world.

When they settled themselves on the sofa with their coffee, she resumed their discussion of the subway homicides. "Have you ever been on a case with so many possible suspects?" she asked.

Ike shook his head. "Never. But what bugs me most about this one is, even with extra detectives on the case, we're not even close to making an arrest."

"Of all the people who might have done it, do you have a favorite?"

He laughed. "A favorite—as in who would I put my money on if I were a betting man?"

"Right."

"At the moment, it's a toss-up between Gund's twin sister and the fedora man," he replied. "But tomorrow it could be someone else." He cast her a grin. "Maybe Mrs. Sinclair."

This case was certainly complex, Liz thought. It was no wonder she'd had that bizarre dream last night. It had almost faded from her mind, but enough of it remained to tell Ike. He'd get a laugh out of it.

"Last night I had the craziest dream," she said. "Gram and her new kitten and all the murder suspects were in my apartment for dinner, but I didn't have any food, and then Paula came in, and right after that you arrived with Aunt Hilda and Chinese takeout."

Ike remained silent for a few moments before drawing her into his arms. "No more homicide talk for the rest of the evening," he said.

"Why?" she asked.

Tightening his embrace, he replied, "When all I do in your dreams is arrive with Chinese takeout and my maiden aunt, it's time for a change."

He didn't have to explain. His kiss said it all.

Chapter Twenty

The next morning, when Liz's alarm clock awakened her, she felt sure her night's sleep had been dreamless. Or if it hadn't, she couldn't remember. It didn't matter anyway, she thought, as she got ready for her day. That last hour before Ike went home was better than anything she could have dreamed.

When she turned on her TV, she noticed that the news coverage of the subway homicides was wearing thin. The victims' funeral services had been covered, and, for lack of new developments, networks and news channels had been running the same footage of possible suspects over and over. Now they were interviewing people who had any kind of connection to the murdered women, no matter how remote.

After viewing a young man whose cousin had once dated Justine Meister's college roommate, Liz wondered

175

how long it would be before some real news broke. When it did, would it be something about the fedora man or twin sister Edwina? Ike seemed to be concentrating mainly on those angles of the case, although he'd jokingly said this could change to include Mrs. Sinclair.

On her way out the door, she recalled Ike's saying he'd be working late for the next couple of days. Never, since she'd known him, had a case tied him up like this.

While she walked to the crosstown bus, Sophie phoned, asking, "How'd your dinner go with Ms. Moneybags?"

Liz described the evening in Paula's lavish apartment.

"Wow," Sophie said. "Vintage wine and catered lobsters. That's going to be a hard act to follow. You owe her a dinner now. How are you going to reciprocate?"

"I'll take her to one of the less expensive Italian or Mexican restaurants. If she hasn't already figured I'm not in her class when it comes to money, that will do it."

"When are you going to pay her back for the catered dinner?"

"I know it should be soon."

"Sounds like an obligation instead of a friendly get-together."

"I guess it is. But I can't help feeling sorry for Paula. With all her wealth, she's kind of pathetic. Most likely I'll see her once in a while. Anyway, even though her chatter about her rich family drives me up a wall, it's better than spending an evening missing Ike."

She paused, looking into the street traffic. "Oh, here comes my bus!"

"We'll talk later," Sophie said.

On the bus, Liz found herself thinking that if she continued to see Paula whenever Ike was busy, it would be like using her. Suddenly, she came close to feeling guilty about being so happy, in love with a wonderful guy and planning their wedding, while Paula was brokenhearted over the man who'd moved away.

Last evening, Paula had seemed to take it for granted there'd be more get-togethers and had appointed *her,* Liz, the official cheerer-upper. Well, chances were, it wouldn't last long. Someone as attractive as Paula wouldn't have to rely on paid escorts forever. Sooner or later she'd meet a nice guy, fall in love, and forget about the one who'd been transferred to California. Until then, bolstering Paula's spirits once in a while could be endured.

During the morning, she decided to phone Paula at work to thank her for the gourmet dinner. If Paula couldn't come to the phone, she'd leave a message. Paula was so down last night about her fizzled romance and her lonely life, even a message might cheer her up.

The veterinarian's receptionist told her Paula was available and put Liz through.

Paula sounded genuinely pleased. "Liz! I was just thinking about you."

"Can you talk for a few minutes?" Liz asked.

"Yes. We just finished delivering a litter of poodles,

and I'm taking a break. I was going to phone you. When I called Lamar to get you a cab last night, he said a man was down there waiting for you. A policeman, he said. Was that your fiancé?"

"Yes. I didn't get around to telling you he's an NYPD detective."

Paula laughed. "I was about to ask why you didn't tell me before that he's a detective, but I didn't give you a chance to tell me *anything,* did I? How are you doing after an evening of hearing about all my troubles?"

Despite the laugh, Liz could tell that Paula was feeling downcast. "The evening was much more than that," she replied, hoping to cheer her up. "The dinner was delicious, and I enjoyed seeing your beautiful apartment and meeting Brutus."

Something close to a groan came over the phone. "Wait till I tell you what happened after you left," Paula said. "Remember I told you the owner of the building lives in the apartment next to mine, and he's been giving me a bad time about Brutus' barking?"

"I remember," Liz replied. She also remembered the earsplitting barks directed at her. They were loud enough to jostle the pictures off the wall of the adjoining apartment.

"Well, he came to my door, complaining again," Paula continued. "Of course Brutus barked when he heard the doorbell, and I had to rush him into the storeroom before I could open the door. Mr. Margolin was even ruder and nastier than usual. Honestly, Liz, I think he must keep his ear to the wall, just waiting for Brutus to bark so he can complain. When I gave up my cat, I thought he'd be satisfied, but . . ." Her voice trailed off.

"Has he threatened to put you out?" Liz asked.

"No, but my lease will be up in a couple of months, and I'm sure he won't renew it. I don't care. I'm fed up with Mr. Margolin. I'm going to move out as soon as possible, even if he charges me for breaking my lease. I'm going to buy a house of my own, where Brutus can bark as much as he wants to. Maybe I'll get another cat."

"A house—here in the city?" Liz asked.

"Oh, yes. I wouldn't think of moving out of Manhattan. I like it here, and I'll like it even more when I get my own house. It hasn't been good for me, living right across the hall from where my ex-boyfriend used to live." Her voice broke. "With Christmas coming, I've been so depressed. I know I was especially down last night. I'm sorry you had to put up with me."

A change of scenery might be exactly what Paula needed, Liz thought. She glanced at her watch. "I have to get back to work, Paula. So long for now," she said.

"So long, Liz."

There was no mistaking the melancholy note in Paula's voice.

Later in the morning, Sophie phoned Liz from her squad car. "I gotta make this quick—we're on our way to break up a domestic fight," she said. "Ralph's working tonight, and I thought if Ike's working, too, we could meet somewhere for dinner and then do some Christmas shopping."

"Sounds good," Liz replied. "I haven't even thought

about Christmas shopping, and it's time I did. Where shall we meet?"

"How about our favorite Rock Center restaurant? There are lots of gift shops around there, and it's handy to the Fifth Avenue stores, too."

"Okay," Liz said. "But this time of the year, that area will be packed with people who've come to see the Rockefeller Center Christmas tree and go skating at the rink. All the eating places will probably be crowded. I'm sure we'll need a reservation. I'll take care of it. I hope they're not booked up."

"I'll do it," Sophie replied. "Remember, the manager is a good friend of Ralph's."

"Oh, that's right. Okay, then—about quarter to six?"

"Yeah. I'll see you then."

Liz hung up the phone, realizing how preoccupied she'd been. Christmas was only two weeks away, and she'd barely given it a thought until now.

She decided to order a sandwich and coffee instead of going out on her lunch break. Eating at her desk would free up some time. She'd make out her Christmas list and be all set to hit the stores with Sophie.

While waiting for her lunch order, she wrote down names, with a suggestion next to each.

Finding gifts for Mom and Pop would be easy. Since they moved to Florida, they'd taken up golf. *Sports shirts,* she wrote next to their names. And a box of Titleists, she thought, adding that. To avoid the mailing hassle, she'd have everything gift-wrapped and sent out from the store.

She wouldn't have to spend much time on Dan, either. As she did every Christmas, she'd give him a subscription to his favorite hunting-and-fishing magazine.

For the others on her list—Gram, Rosa and Joe, Sophie and Ralph, and especially Ike—it wouldn't be that simple. She'd have to do some serious thinking and a lot of legwork. It couldn't all be accomplished tonight.

And what about Ike's family? Of course Ike would get something for them, but should she also buy gifts for them all? Perhaps she and Ike should give each member of his family a joint gift. She'd have to talk this over with Ike. He'd be working again tomorrow night, but maybe by Thursday there'd be a break in the case, and they'd have some time together.

That evening, when Liz got off the uptown subway and headed west toward Fifth Avenue, she noticed that the area was more crowded than usual. This crisp, clear night so close to Christmas had brought a lot of people into the city, she thought. The streets and walkways in the vicinity of Rockefeller Center were jammed with pedestrians, most of them carrying packages. Everyone seemed to be in a holiday mood, she thought, as she crossed the avenue and approached the plaza, where the famous Rockefeller Center Christmas tree stood in all its glory.

Shouldering her way through the dense crowd on the sidewalk leading to the restaurant, she knew that every eatery in the area would be packed, and people would be lined up, waiting for tables. Lucky the manager of the restaurant where she and Sophie were to meet was a buddy of Ralph's, she thought, when suddenly a grim idea struck her. If the subway killer changed his MO, this would be an ideal setting for another murder.

Although she'd speculated about that and even warned Paula, the idea had lacked substance. Now, as she made her way along the crammed sidewalk, jostled and buffeted by the crowd, it became all too real.

She glanced around her. Most of the women she saw were bareheaded. Others wore headgear from which their hair hung out in plain view.

A feeling of apprehension gripped her. What if the man in the fedora was on the prowl in Rockefeller Center tonight? *Somewhere on these crowded streets there could be a red-haired woman too caught up in the holiday spirit to be careful, or who believed the killer would only strike on the subway during mild weather.*

Last week's springlike temperatures were gone. Women had packed away their light jackets and sweaters and gone into winter wear. Hoping to ease her apprehension, she tried to convince herself that the killer wouldn't switch his operations from the subway to some other crowded place while the weather was cold. He'd figure a potential victim would be wearing heavy clothing. She wanted to believe he wouldn't risk botching the job.

Her efforts didn't work. Instead, she told herself the killer would use a needle more capable of penetrating the sleeve of a heavy coat.

By the time she got to the restaurant, her feelings of apprehension had intensified. Sophie had not yet arrived, but all she had to do was mention Ralph's name, and she was shown to a table. She ordered a glass of

Merlot to calm herself before Sophie arrived. If she didn't settle down, Sophie would notice. She hoped word of the man in the fedora had gotten out around the station house so she and Sophie could talk about it. But at least Ike had given her the okay to tell Sophie that her original idea had evolved into a strong possibility.

"Sorry I'm late," Sophie said, sliding into the opposite chair. "How about that crowd out there? Christmas shoppers and tourists are out in droves."

"It's a beautiful night," Liz replied. "Cold enough to feel Christmassy, but no snow or ice to keep people home. I hope the stores won't be too crowded."

Sophie picked up a menu. "Guess we'd better eat and get to our shopping." She eyed Liz's wineglass. "And I'll join you with some of that."

While they ate, Liz decided to tell Sophie that Ike liked her revenge-on-all-red-haired-women theory. "Ike picked up your idea that the subway killer might be going after redheads because he has an insane grudge against a red-haired woman," she said.

Sophie gave a pleased smile. "Yeah? He really thinks there's something to it?"

Liz nodded and related her own idea about a red-haired nanny in the Sinclair household. "Ike's going to look into it."

"A red-haired nanny—that's a good one," Sophie said. "This idea has a bunch of angles, like a mean school-teacher or stepmother, or a redhead who left him at the altar."

"Or maybe kept him from achieving his life's goal," Liz added.

"Oh, that's another good one," Sophie said. "A red-haired woman got the promotion he was up for. But I like your idea of the redhead nanny best."

"I don't think Mama Sinclair would have done the killing herself," Liz said. "She probably hired a hit man."

"That's good, too," Sophie said. "But why would the hit man kill the other two women?"

"Maybe Mrs. Sinclair was so psychotic about red-haired women that she offered him a bonus for every other redhead he eliminated," Liz replied.

They both burst out laughing. When she and Sophie started speculating, they always had fun coming up with far-fetched concepts, Liz thought.

But this last idea could also hold true for Eddie Gund's twin sister, she thought. Edwina Gund could have hired someone to bump off the red-haired woman she believed would break her brother's heart, plus as many other pretty young redheads as possible.

She was about to suggest this to Sophie when Sophie broke in with yet another speculation. "What if the murderer's wife was killed in a car crash, and the driver of the other car was a drunken red-haired woman?"

The discussion was starting to bring back Liz's earlier apprehensive feelings. "Let's get off the subway killer and talk about our shopping," she said. "Do you have any idea what you're going to give Ralph for Christmas?"

Sophie nodded. "I'm thinking about a nice wallet. I noticed the one he has is getting ratty. Have you decided what to give Ike?"

"No, but a wallet sounds like a good idea," Liz

replied. "Ike's looks like it was a present when he graduated from high school."

"Let's go to that shop near here that has luggage and leather stuff," Sophie said.

In the luggage shop, they found handsome wallets for Ike and Ralph. Liz also bought a fashionably large purse for Gram.

"To carry her winnings home from those senior citizen bus trips to Atlantic City," she told Sophie with a laugh.

Sophie was delighted to find a designer purse for her sister, on sale. "Teenage girls can be very picky, but this is something I know Debbie will go for," she said.

In a bookstore, Liz bought a cookbook for Rosa to add to her large collection, and a book for Joe authored by a Marine Corps general.

Sophie bought a gardening book for her mother-in-law, a best-selling novel for her mother, and a how-to book on home improvement for her father. "He'll love this, and so will Ma," she said. "They've been talking about remodeling the kitchen."

By now they were laden with bags, and Sophie suggested they call it quits on the shopping for the night. "We can do this again at least once more before Christmas," she said.

"Right," Liz agreed. "And let's take a taxi home."

Sophie nodded. "Lucky we live near each other. Splitting the fare, it won't cost either of us too much. Let's walk over to Fifth Avenue, where there'll be plenty of taxis."

They got a cab right away and had just started off when Liz's phone sounded.

"I'll bet that's Ike," she said, digging the phone out of her purse.

It was. "Where are you?" he asked.

"In a taxi with Sophie. We're on our way home from Christmas shopping in Rock Center."

He didn't reply. "Are you there, Ike?" she asked.

"Yeah. I'm through working. I'll meet you at your place."

Something in his voice alerted her senses. *Had her earlier apprehensions materialized? Had the subway killer changed his MO tonight and struck down another red-haired victim in some other crowded place?*

She hoped he might drop a hint. "Did something happen with the subway homicides tonight?"

"I'll tell you all about it when I see you," he replied.

Chapter Twenty-one

"I could tell by like's voice, something's up with the subway homicides," Liz said.

"Do you suppose they've made an arrest?" Sophie asked.

Liz shook her head. "He didn't sound upbeat. I think the killer might have struck again."

Sophie looked surprised. "Would he have risked it, with cops riding the trains, plus everyone wearing heavy clothing?"

"He might have decided to operate in some other crowded place, and maybe he got a needle that would penetrate heavy clothing," Liz replied. "And that mob scene in Rockefeller Center would have been an ideal place for a change of MO."

"Yeah," Sophie said with a nod. "Redheaded women who'd been wearing hats or scarves on the subway might think they didn't have to be careful in other places."

When the cab drew close to Sophie's apartment building, Sophie started to gather up her packages. "I'll call you at work tomorrow," she said, alighting at the building's entrance. "By then, whatever happened tonight might be all over the news."

And whatever it was, like would tell her when he got to her place, Liz thought, while the taxi drove on to the Moscarettis' brownstone.

Rosa greeted her in the lower hall, handing her an envelope, saying, "Hello, dearie. You got your electric bill." Eyeing Liz's packages, she added, "Looks like you've been Christmas shopping."

"I have," Liz replied on her way up the stairs. "I bought a neat purse for Gram, among other things."

"Is Ike dropping by later?" Rosa asked.

"He'll be here in a few minutes."

"He's been working long hours these days, hasn't he?"

"Yes, he has," Liz replied from the top of the stairs. Ordinarily she would have lingered to chat with Rosa, but now she wanted to have coffee ready for Ike when he got there.

"Well, I'll see you tomorrow when you get home from work," Rosa called.

"Right," Liz called in return.

She had barely enough time to freshen up and put the coffee on before Ike arrived. After giving her a hug and a kiss, he glanced toward the kitchenette with an appreciative smile. "I smell coffee. Good!"

"Are you hungry?" she asked. "I could fix you a sandwich."

"Thanks, but we grabbed something about an hour ago."

He followed her behind the bamboo screen, where she poured the coffee.

"Please don't keep me in suspense," she said, handing him his mug and heading for the sofa. "What's up with the case?"

When they were settled, he took a generous swallow of coffee before setting the mug down on a side table. "Okay," he said. "There was an incident tonight, in the crowd outside Radio City Music Hall."

Liz held back a gasp. *The Music Hall was only two blocks away from where she and Sophie ate dinner!*

"A young, red-haired woman reported being jostled and felt something being poked at her arm," Ike continued. "Fortunately, she quickly turned away."

"Did she see the person who jostled her?" Liz asked,

"Yeah. She got a good look at him when she turned around and pulled away from him, before he disappeared into the crowd. She was able to give a fairly good description. She said he had a dark complexion and a dark mustache and—"

Liz's could not keep from interrupting. "And he was wearing a brown felt hat with a wide brim turned down over his eyes?"

"Right. Looks as if the fedora man, whoever he is, is the killer."

"Don't laugh," Liz said, "but when I saw those crowds in Rockefeller Center tonight, I got a strong feeling that the killer might be prowling around that area, looking for another redhead."

"I'm not laughing," Ike replied. "Imagine how I felt when you told me you'd been shopping in Rockefeller Center tonight."

"But with my brown hair, I wouldn't have been a target," she reminded him.

He drew her into a hug. "I know, but when I'm not with you, I keep forgetting. I always think of you with beautiful red hair before I remember you're a safe brown."

" 'Safe brown' sounds dull and drab," she said. "I wish you'd hurry up and catch this killer."

"Me, too," he replied. "You're a long way from dull and drab, but I want my red-haired sweetheart back."

She gave him an appreciative kiss. "I guess this woman tonight wasn't wearing a head covering," she said.

"Right. According to the report, she didn't think the subway killer would be operating anywhere but on the six train."

That's because the news media had labeled him as such, Liz thought. *The subway killer.* How many other young red-haired women had been lulled into a false sense of security by that?

"I hope news of this gets out before he attacks another redhead in an area nowhere near the subway," she said. "The next one might not be as quick to sense danger."

Ike glanced toward the TV. "There should be a bulletin out by now."

She picked up the remote. "I got so tired of the repeated coverage and the dumb interviews, I stopped watching," she said, turning it on.

A bulletin on the incident near Rockefeller Center was just starting. Listening to the commentator deliver the report, Liz realized there was no mention of a man in a fedora. She remembered Ike's saying he hoped the news media wouldn't get hold of that information.

"Looks as if those subway witnesses haven't blabbed about seeing a man in a big felt hat," she said.

Ike nodded. "Let's hope they don't. We want to keep that information restricted as long as possible so as not to alert the killer that we're wise to it. It's enough that the public has been informed of this thwarted attack and Manhattan's red-haired women now know they're not safe anywhere in the city with their hair exposed."

"That woman was lucky," Liz said.

"Yeah, and she played it cool. She said the instant she felt the jostle against her arm, she realized the danger and quickly pulled back and got out of his way before she was jabbed. She didn't scream or anything. She just made her way out of the crowd and headed for the nearest police station. But best of all, she didn't let on to the killer that she'd gotten a look at him."

Smart lady, Liz thought. With the report of the thwarted attack now on the news, the fedora man would know the woman had reported it, but as far as he knew, she hadn't described her assailant as wearing a wide-brimmed felt hat. No mention of the hat had been made public. That could mean he'd continue wearing it while roaming the city in his quest for more red-haired women to kill. The longer he remained unaware that his hat had been noticed, the sooner he'd be captured.

"We're beefing up surveillance in all the most crowded areas throughout Manhattan," Ike said. "We'll get him."

"Does this mean you've given up on the other possible suspects?" Liz asked.

Ike shook his head emphatically. "Absolutely not. We're keeping all our irons in the fire."

Ike might suspect that one of the men on the persons-of-interest list might be the fedora man, Liz thought. In addition to Bernie Weiss, visions flashed in her head of Marco Denali or Giles Sinclair skulking around Manhattan, wearing a felt hat with the brim pulled down over his eyes.

But whatever vivid fancies her imagination created, they all paled when the familiar question arose: *Why had he killed three red-haired women, and why was he going after more?*

Ike's phone sounded. "Sorry," he said, taking it out of his pocket.

She picked up his coffee mug and took it to the kitchenette for a refill, feeling sure when she returned he'd tell her what the call was about. At the coffeemaker, an exciting thought popped into her mind: *Could the killer have been caught?*

When she brought Ike his coffee, he was off the phone, but one look at his face told her the call had not borne good news. "What happened?" she asked.

"Tonight's incident outside the Music Hall has the DA in a furor," he replied. "He's itchy for an arrest."

This wasn't the first time a district attorney had pressured city police detectives, Liz thought. She recalled a recent case where an elderly house servant had been charged with the murder of his wealthy employer, solely on the grounds that he'd been left a generous sum of money. Liz had been partially responsible for Ike's apprehending the actual killer before the case went to trial. That was the first time she'd provided Ike with a clue. The case had brought them together.

That particular DA was a highly ambitious politician who'd been running for reelection. The present one was not. She was surprised that this one would lean on Ike this way. From what she knew about him, he was a man of integrity.

"This case has been rough on the DA," Ike said. "He's getting a lot of pressure from citizens and civic groups demanding action."

"Has he given you a deadline?"

"Not exactly, but he asked that we redouble our efforts and try to get it wrapped up before the New Year," Ike replied. "He doesn't want this to turn into another Son of Sam case."

"That gives us only a couple of weeks," Liz said.

Ike flashed a teasing grin. *"Us?"*

He followed with a quick kiss. "Just kidding, Redlocks. I know you're into this case almost as deeply as I am."

He got to his feet, saying he had to leave and he'd be working again the next night. "I won't be able to make it for dinner, but maybe I can stop by later for a little while. I'll give you a call."

Chapter Twenty-two

The next morning, Sophie phoned Liz at work. "I was going to call you last night, but I knew Ike was there," she said. "I caught the bulletin on TV. Can you believe an attempt to kill another redhead happened while we were in the restaurant only a couple of blocks away?"

"And while we were talking about the possibility of a change in his MO," Liz added. "The news channels are full of it this morning. But at least it's something new."

"I'm sure Ike told you that plainclothes cops have been assigned to the most crowded areas."

"Right, he did."

"And there's buzz around the station house that they're keeping their eyes peeled for a guy in a wide-brimmed felt hat."

Good, Liz thought. The uniforms had the word. Now she could discuss it freely with Sophie. "According to

Ike, the woman who reported last night's incident said the man who jostled her was wearing a hat like that."

"I guess as long as there's nothing on the news about it, he'll feel safe wearing it," Sophie said. A moment later she said she had to hang up. "We gotta go break up a street fight," she said.

Later in the day, Ike called. "Looks like a long, busy night," he said. "I don't know what time I'll be quitting, and I don't like keeping you up waiting for me."

He shouldn't have to be concerned about that, she thought. He had enough on his mind. "I can survive another evening without being together if you can," she said with a laugh. "When the case is solved, we'll get in some quality time."

"You can count on that," he replied. "I'll call you tonight when I'm finished working, unless I think it's too late and you might be asleep."

"Feel free to wake me up," Liz said.

When Liz got home that evening, Rosa greeted her in the entrance hall, as usual. "No mail for you except this circular, dearie," she said. "Shall I throw it away?"

As Liz nodded, Rosa suddenly glanced up the stairway, saying, "I think I hear your phone, dearie. Better run and get it. Maybe it's Ike."

Liz felt sure it wasn't Ike. *Unless there'd been a huge break in the case.* She hurried up to her apartment. Grabbing the phone, she noticed the caller ID. It was Sophie.

"Liz, I just found out that Ralph has to go to a meeting tonight. He won't be home for dinner. If Ike's working, maybe we could get together."

"Oh, good! Ike's tied up until late again, and I wasn't looking forward to another solitary evening. Shall we meet somewhere, or what?"

"We haven't been to our favorite Italian restaurant for ages," Sophie replied. "Let's meet there, say, in an hour?"

"Fine." Liz hung up the phone with a smile. Another empty evening averted, and spending it with Sophie was the next best thing to spending it with Ike. The restaurant was within walking distance of both their apartments; the food was good and the prices reasonable.

She'd just turned on the TV to catch whatever news about the case might be on, when her phone rang again. Could it be Ike saying he could make it for dinner, after all?

Instead of Ike's voice, Paula's came over the phone. She sounded agitated. "Liz, I would have called you at your job, but you never told me where you worked, so I waited till I thought you'd be home."

"Hello, Paula. I just got home a few minutes ago."

Of course Paula had heard the bulletin about the subway killer in Rockefeller Center, Liz thought. That's why she was calling. "I guess you were stunned when you heard the subway killer tried to get another redhead last night, weren't you, Paula?"

"Yes, I was stunned, and I'm terribly upset. It was exactly like you told me. He changed his MO. I'm so grateful to you for warning me, Liz, and for insisting that I hide my hair. Suppose you hadn't? If I happened to be near Radio City Music Hall last night, that woman could have been me, and I might not have been so lucky. I'm so thankful I listened to you. That's one reason I called—to say thanks, and also I heard on the news that the District Attorney has ordered more detectives on the case and more overtime. I thought your fiancé might be working tonight and you could go out to dinner with me. I'm so shook up about this, I need company."

Liz suppressed a sigh. "Oh, Paula, I'm sorry, but I have plans for dinner tonight."

"Isn't your fiancé on the case?"

"Yes, but I'm having dinner with a woman friend."

Just as she feared, Paula wasn't going to take no for an answer.

"Can't you get out of it?"

"Sorry, Paula, I can't."

"Oh, come on, Liz . . ."

Liz was starting to feel annoyed. "Please don't argue with me about this, Paula."

After several silent moments, Paula spoke again. "Is this woman friend around our age?"

"Yes. Why do you ask?"

"As long as she's not some old dowager, how about the three of us having dinner together? Have you decided where you're going to eat? I'll meet you there, or I could pick both of you up in my taxi and take you to the restaurant, then take you home from there after dinner."

Get-togethers with Sophie were few enough these days. Paula's presence would put a damper on this one. Instead of indulging in their usual gab, they'd have to listen to Paula talk about her money.

She took a deep breath. "Paula, having dinner with you tonight is definitely out."

Hoping to soften her rather harsh statement, she added, "But you and I will plan something very soon. My treat. I haven't forgotten that scrumptious dinner at your place."

Something like a sob came over the phone. "Oh, Liz, I'm terribly upset tonight. I need company."

Liz was tempted to suggest she call the escort service but refrained. Paula seemed too distraught to handle sarcasm. She was wondering how she could say good-bye without evoking more sobs, when she found herself thinking, what if, after they hung up, Paula polished off two or three goblets of wine and then called the escort service for her favorite guy, the one she'd been with in the restaurant? Even though Ike thought she was too sophisticated to fall for a con man's line, the wine, plus her state of mind, might make her vulnerable.

She'd just succeeded in convincing herself that she should not feel responsible for Paula's actions, when another possible scenario popped into her mind. She pictured Paula washing down a handful of sleeping pills with half a bottle of wine.

That possibility was something she could not easily ignore. Reluctantly, she gave in.

"Okay, Paula." She gave the address of the restaurant. "We'll meet you there in about an hour."

"Oh, thank you, thank you, Liz! I don't think I could have gotten through this evening alone," Paula exclaimed.

Liz started feeling guilty about being harsh with her, when Paula suddenly switched from grateful to critical. "But I've never heard of that restaurant. I hope it isn't one of those cheap family eating places with kids and babies in high chairs smearing spaghetti all over themselves," she said.

Liz seized the chance to keep Paula from joining them. "Actually, that's pretty much what it is," she replied.

"Couldn't we meet somewhere else?" Paula asked, sounding petulant. "If you want pasta, I know a wonderful, upscale Italian restaurant."

"My friend expects me to meet her where we planned, and I can't get in touch with her," Liz lied. "She's out somewhere, and she doesn't have a cell phone."

"Oh, all right," Paula replied, somewhat crossly. "I'll call my cab driver, and we'll pick you up."

"Thanks, Paula, but the restaurant is only a short walk from here."

"Why walk when you can ride?" Paula asked. She hung up before Liz could reply.

Liz called Sophie immediately and told her about Paula's horning in. "I tried to head her off, but no luck. She's all upset about what happened near Rockefeller Center last night and says she needs company."

Sophie didn't seem to mind. "That's okay. It'll give me a chance to meet Ms. Moneybags."

When Liz got into Paula's cab, she noticed Paula's ultrachic outfit right away. She had on a long, camel-colored suede coat over black pants and a black turtleneck. Every lock of her hair was securely bundled under a black silk turban, from which dangled gold hoop earrings.

Liz made no comment on the outfit, especially the earrings. She didn't want to hear Paula brag that they were twenty-carat gold. Instead, she gave an approving nod at the turban.

"I'm glad to see you're hiding your hair, Paula."

"After what happened last night, I knew I had to," Paula replied. "Thanks for letting me join you tonight, Liz. I've been so terribly upset, but I'm beginning to feel better, now that I don't have to eat dinner alone."

She was in her pathetic mode again, Liz thought. Well, that was preferable to her bragging.

Sophie was already in the restaurant at a table. She rose to greet them, all smiles.

"So, you're Paula," she said, without waiting for Liz to introduce them. "It's such a pleasure to meet you. I'm Sophie. Liz has told me so much about you. I'm delighted to have you join us."

Liz could barely keep a straight face. Anyone hearing Sophie gush like this would never believe she'd dubbed Paula Ms. Moneybags.

"Hello, Sophie, thanks for including me," Paula said, sitting down and casting a disapproving glance around the neat but very plain restaurant. Although there was only one table with a baby in a high chair, that was enough to bring a frown to her face.

They scanned the menus. "I'm having the eggplant parmesan. It's very good here," Liz said.

"So's the rigatoni with clam sauce," Sophie added. "That's what I'm having."

Liz looked at Paula. "Actually, you can't go wrong with whatever you order here."

Looking slightly dubious, Paula said she'd order lasagna.

She picked up the wine list, looking as if she didn't expect to find anything there up to her standards. "What wine do you usually order?" she asked.

"Chianti," Sophie and Liz chorused. They didn't add that it was an okay wine, reasonably priced.

After they ordered, Paula turned to Sophie, saying, "I'm sure Liz told you I'm terribly upset tonight."

Sophie nodded. "Yeah. She told me the incident near Rock Center last night really got to you."

Paula nodded. "But it's not only that . . ." She looked at Liz. "I wasn't going to tell you this, Liz, because I didn't want to worry you, but I've got to get it off my chest. Last time I went out with Kyle, my favorite, he made a remark that scared me."

"Favorite?" Sophie asked, as if Liz hadn't told her about the escort service.

Paula hesitated for a moment before replying. "Please don't think I'm foolish, Sophie, but I've been so lonesome since my boyfriend's company transferred him to California, I've been going out with men who get paid for escorting women to the theatre and restaurants and so forth."

"Oh, my," Sophie replied, putting on a shocked face.

"I knew that would surprise you," Paula continued, "but it's really helping me get through a bad time. I ask for one of them, Kyle, often, because he's by far the best-looking and most sophisticated man at the escort service. I liked him until he made a scary remark."

Liz was about to ask what Kyle had said, when Sophie beat her to it.

"What was the scary remark?"

"Well, we were talking about the subway murders, when Kyle said that if he were the killer, I wouldn't have a thing to worry about, because he knew I wasn't a natural redhead."

"Don't you think he was just kidding?" Liz asked.

Paula didn't seem to hear the question. She was already looking at Liz and Sophie, glancing from one to the other, asking, "Does my hair look dyed to you? Can you tell I'm not a real redhead?"

Liz thought she seemed more concerned about that than about Kyle's remark. "I thought your red hair was natural," she replied. She told herself the lie was justified. Why get Paula more upset than she already was?

Sophie peered at Paula's turban. "I haven't seen your hair, but if Liz thinks it looks natural, I guess it does."

"That makes me feel better," Paula said. "But I don't want Kyle for an escort anymore. Ever since he said that, I've been wondering if he—" Abruptly, she cut off whatever words she would have spoken, saying instead, "Let's talk about something else."

Liz glanced at Sophie. She glanced back. They were both thinking the same thing, Liz decided. Paula thought that Kyle might be the subway killer.

Following Paula's suggestion, they changed the subject. Paula did most of the talking. She launched into a lengthy dissertation, telling Sophie all about her affluent life on the family's ranch in Oklahoma, and how the Rubiks were financially right up there with the Rockefellers.

Having heard it all before, Liz turned her mind back to Kyle, the paid escort. Could he possibly be the man out to kill as many pretty, young, red-haired women as he could?

But the police were looking for a swarthy man with a mustache, wearing a brown fedora with the brim pulled down. In her mind's eye, she pictured Kyle as she'd seen him in the restaurant with Paula. Although his hair was dark, his complexion hadn't impressed her as swarthy, and he had no mustache.

They finished eating. Paula said she'd call her cab driver and give them both a lift home.

"I feel so much better," she told them, while they waited for her driver. "Thank you for letting me join you."

In the cab, Sophie said her apartment was on the way to Liz's, and the driver could let her off first.

"I've enjoyed meeting you, Sophie," Paula said, as the driver maneuvered the cab through the traffic. "Thanks again to both of you for letting me horn in on your dinner. We should do this again, soon, only next time we'll get together at my apartment. I want you to see it, Sophie. It's really posh, right, Liz?"

Liz scarcely had time to nod before Paula continued chattering. "But I've started looking for a house to buy, and it's going to be even more luxurious than where I am now. I looked at one absolutely gorgeous house I've almost decided on. I'm going to see it again, and I'll probably make an offer. Of course it's terribly expensive, but I have more than enough money to buy it."

It was as if she'd forgotten all about Kyle and his frightening remark, Liz thought. But that was Paula. Her moods varied even more than her glamorous outfits.

After they'd dropped Sophie off, Paula remarked that

Sophie seemed very nice. "Have you known her long, Liz?" she asked.

"Only since we were six years old," Liz replied with a laugh.

"I can't imagine being friends with someone for so many years," Paula said.

While Liz was thinking that was an odd remark, Paula started to explain it. "I mean, people change as time passes. I'm not friends with any of the girls I knew in Oklahoma. But Sophie's very nice, although a bit of a prig. Did you notice how shocked she looked when I told her about the escort service?"

Hearing Sophie described as a prig almost made Liz laugh out loud. She was about to tell Paula that Sophie was a cop, when Paula spoke again.

"Enough about Sophie. I want to hear more about your detective fiancé. What does he look like? Tall, dark, and handsome?"

Liz found herself mellowing. "Tall, *blond,* and handsome," she replied.

"Oh," Paula said. "There was a tall, blond detective investigating drug thefts in Dr. Jurgens' office not long ago. I didn't catch his name. I wonder if he could have been your guy."

Liz smiled. "That was Ike. He told me about being there. Matter of fact, he told me about the litter of kittens. That's how I got the kitten for my grandmother."

"He's good-looking, all right," Paula replied. "You're so lucky, Liz." Suddenly she looked as if she had just recalled something. "I overhead him telling Dr. Jurgens that he was working on the subway murders."

Liz nodded. "That's right. He's a homicide detective."

"Well, I hope he catches that killer soon," Paula said. "I don't want to spend the rest of my life with my hair bundled under a turban."

"And I don't want to spend the rest of *my* life with brown hair instead of my own strawberry blond," Liz replied.

Paula looked at her, obviously surprised. "Strawberry blond! You mean you dyed your hair?"

"Right. I did it so the subway killer wouldn't notice me."

"How come you didn't tell me before?" Paula asked. A second later, she laughed. "I know why. Ever since we met, I've talked too much about myself. You couldn't get a word in edgewise."

She laughed again. "What a pair we are! You dyed your red hair brown, and I dyed my brown hair red. But strawberry blond is such a pretty shade. How could you bring yourself to do it?"

"It was Ike's idea."

She heard a wistful note in Paula's voice. "Your Ike looks out for you, doesn't he?"

"Yes, he does," Liz replied, just as the cab drew up in front of the Moscarettis' brownstone.

"Maybe, when I move to my new house, I'll meet a man who'll look after *me,*" Paula replied.

On the way up the stairs to her apartment, Paula's parting words lingered in Liz's mind. Paula needed male companionship more than she needed a fancy house. Getting settled would keep her happily occupied for a while, but soon her life would be as empty as it was before.

When the phone rang, she was sure it would be Sophie, wanting to talk about the evening with Ms. Moneybags. It was.

"She's a character, all right," Sophie said. "Cranky one minute and sweet as pie the next. And all that talk about her money. Seems like that's all she has in her life. I couldn't help feeling sorry for her."

"Me, too," Liz replied. "I thought at first we could strike up a friendship, but lately, like you, I just pity her."

After saying good-bye to Sophie, she turned on the TV to watch the news. After reports about the latest celebrity divorces, arrests for DUI, and rehab releases, a bulletin came on. A newscaster announced that a swarthy young man wearing a wide-brimmed hat had been noticed in the subway in the same time frames when each of the three red-haired women had been attacked.

The news that Ike had hoped would remain quiet for a while was now out.

Chapter Twenty-three

Although Ike had told her this would eventually leak out, it still came as something of a shock. If the fedora man were, indeed, the subway killer, he'd soon know that the public had a description of him. Now he'd be even more difficult to find. He certainly wouldn't be roaming through crowded areas in a fedora anymore, with a syringe ready to jab into the arm of the first redhead he encountered. He might even go into hiding.

That would be discouraging for Ike, she thought. A big part of his investigation would be slowed up. Had he heard about it yet?

As if in answer, her phone rang. "Are you watching TV?" Ike asked.

"Yes. I caught the bulletin. I'm sorry this happened."

To her surprise, he didn't seem glum. "It was in the

cards," he said. "Besides, now it's unlikely that there'll be any more murders or attempted murders of red-haired women for a while."

Liz thought this sounded as if Ike were sure the fedora man was the killer. A moment later she recalled the strange remark the paid escort had made about Paula's hair.

"I have something I need to run by you," she said. "And not over the phone."

"Something to do with the case?"

"Yes, but I'm not sure if you'll think there's anything to it. Could you come over tomorrow night, even if it's very late?"

"I can do better than that," he said. "I'm on my way home, and I'm not far from your place. I was just going to ask you if it's too late for me to drop by tonight. I have something for you."

She barely had time to put her old plaid flannel robe on over her pajamas, slip her feet into the furry slippers she'd had since her college days, and comb her hair, before the entry buzzer sounded from downstairs. She hurried to answer.

"Ike?"

"Yeah. Are you sure this isn't too late for you to be receiving a male caller?" She could tell by his voice, he was teasing.

"Not when the caller is my favorite NYPD detective," she replied. "I must warn you, though, I'm not what you'd call *dressed*."

"Coming right up," he said.

Seconds later he was there, giving her a hug and a kiss, and appraising the plaid robe, saying, "Not exactly Victoria's Secret, but I like it."

"Lucky you do," she replied. "In a few weeks you'll be seeing it every night."

"That can't come soon enough," he said, drawing her onto the sofa and giving her another kiss. "I hope this damn case will be wrapped up before our wedding day. We don't want to start our married life with me working late every night." In the next moment he added, "But not much chance of that. The DA wants an arrest before New Year's, and I intend to deliver. Now, you said you have something to tell me."

She nodded. "I wish it would turn out to be a big clue, but it's probably nothing. I just thought you should know about it."

"Let's hear it."

"It's about the paid escort we saw with Paula in the restaurant."

"Kyle Bernardo," Ike said.

"I forgot you'd know his name from his arrest," she said.

"So, what about him?"

"Paula told me she wasn't going to ask for him anymore because he said something to her that made her feel uncomfortable. He said if he were the subway killer, he wouldn't go after her, because he could tell she's not a natural redhead. Don't you think that was a strange remark?"

"Yeah, not something a man ordinarily says to a woman. When did Paula tell you this?"

"This evening. Sophie and I had dinner with her. So, what are your thoughts on what Kyle said?"

"If he was just a regular guy, he could have been joking, but a remark like that seems out of character for a man who's being paid to be charming."

Liz told him how Paula had stopped short of saying she thought Kyle might be the subway killer.

Ike was silent for a few moments. "This might bear looking into," he said.

"Does that mean you think there's a possibility Kyle could be the fedora man?" she asked. With a shake of her head, she answered her own question. "But if the killer wears that kind of hat to hide his squinty eyes, then Kyle's not . . ." A sudden thought popped into her mind. "And he doesn't have a mustache, either."

"Neither does Bernie," Ike said teasingly. "But we haven't eliminated the possibility that this guy is just making sure he won't be recognized," Ike replied. "The mustache might be a fake."

Liz nodded. "I should have thought of that. With a fake mustache and the hat brim pulled down to his eyes, he wouldn't be easy to recognize. But you'd think he'd realize that a man wearing an oversized hat like that would stand out like a sore thumb."

Ike gave a wry smile. "He realizes that now."

"I'm sorry it leaked out about the fedora," she said.

"Actually, it's taken some of the pressure off. With the killer alerted, he won't strike again right away."

"Do you think he'll go at it again after a while, wearing a different kind of hat?" Liz asked.

"We haven't ruled that out," he replied. He drew her

into a hug. "Thanks for telling me about Kyle's remark. We'll follow up on it."

She gave a regretful sigh. "I was hoping this would be helpful, but I'm afraid I've only added one more person to your list."

"Leave no stone unturned," he said.

Suddenly he slapped at his coat pocket. "I almost forgot what I have for you."

And she'd been so absorbed in talking about the paid escort's strange remark that she'd forgotten, too. "What is it?" she asked.

He took an envelope out of his pocket. "A letter from Aunt Hilda, sent by Express Mail. It's for both of us." He handed her an envelope.

Liz read the letter through.

My dear Elizabeth and George.

This is to tell you that I have done a lot of thinking since Elizabeth's visit, and I have decided to change my mind and attend your wedding. And I shall reinstate George's bequest. I realize that I have allowed my long-ago unhappy romance to influence my life. I became an angry, bitter old woman. In trying to keep George from marrying you, Elizabeth, I thought I would be getting even. I was trying to do to you what had been done to me so many years ago.

I should have known it wouldn't work. We Eichles can be stubborn as mules, but there's not a wimp anywhere in the line. The letter was signed *Great-aunt Hilda Eichle.*

Liz looked at Ike with a big smile. "I can't believe it!"

"It's almost unbelievable," he agreed. "I never thought

she'd ever set foot in a Catholic church, let alone keep me in her will."

"She's a dear. I'm going to put her letter into our wedding scrapbook."

"Sure, keep it as a memento of how you turned a bitter old lady's mind around," Ike said. He laughed. "And you turned her life around, too. Next to never setting foot in a Catholic church, I didn't believe she'd ever get a TV. But when I talked to Dad today, he said she'd bought one, and would you believe she's been following the subway murders?"

"Really?" Liz asked. "While I was there, we talked a little about my following murder cases and Gram's helping me. I recall she seemed interested, but I never thought she'd get a TV and start following the subway murders. I wonder who's her prime suspect."

"According to Dad, she thinks Bernie Weiss did it," Ike replied. "She's sure he's insane."

"Do you agree with her?" Liz asked with a laugh.

"There's no doubt in my mind that this killer is insane," Ike said. "But, whoever he is, like many insane people, he could also be clever—maybe too clever to tip his hand."

"You mean if Bernie's the killer, he'd keep his intense dislike for Chloe to himself?"

"Right. Chances are, if he were the guilty one, he wouldn't go on TV with an angry tirade against her."

"Are you saying Bernie's off the list of possible suspects?"

Ike shook his head emphatically. "It's too soon to scratch anyone off the list."

Although she disliked pumping him for information, curiosity got the better of her. "Is anyone first on your own, personal list?" she asked.

"It varies from day to day," he replied. "Sometimes even moment to moment," he added with a grin.

Before she could ask him who topped his list at this moment, he glanced at his watch, saying, "It's time I shoved off and let you get some sleep."

Liz stayed awake for quite a while after Ike left. Telling her which of the possible suspects was first on his own list wouldn't have divulged classified information. Why had he been so evasive?

She fell asleep before she could think of an answer.

Chapter Twenty-four

The next morning, when Liz turned on her favorite TV news channel, a commentator was delivering a re-hash. Police were seeking a man wearing a brown felt hat, known as a fedora, with a wide brim. Previous coverage was now modified to state only that the man had been seen in the Lexington Avenue local subway on the same days that the three red-haired women had met with their fatal attacks. Persons seeing a man wearing a hat of this description and acting suspiciously anywhere in the city were asked to notify the NYPD immediately. A phone number was flashed onto the screen.

If the fedora man watched TV or listened to radio or read newspaper headlines, he wouldn't be wandering around the city wearing his big hat, Liz thought, as she got ready to leave for work.

When she passed the Moscarettis' apartment on

her way out, the door opened, and Rosa appeared, all smiles.

"Good news, dearie. Your new apartment will be vacated sooner than we expected. Mr. Klein told us last night he's moving out next week. That means Joe can start painting and fixing it nice for you and Ike right away."

"Oh, that's great, Rosa!" Liz exclaimed.

She and Ike had seen the apartment only once, when Rosa had asked Mr. Klein if they could look at it and get an idea of how much furniture they'd need to buy. The old gentleman had been very obliging and even offered them a yardstick to measure the bedroom wall space.

"I know from my daughter that young people today buy king-size beds and television sets for their bedrooms," he'd said. "When this house was built, there was such thing as king-size beds or TV. You didn't need so much wall space back then."

Mr. Klein had been the Moscarettis' tenant since they'd bought the old brownstone and converted it into apartments, nearly twenty years ago. His accumulation of furnishings and clutter made it difficult to measure, but she and Ike had managed to do it and found there'd be enough room for what they wanted to buy.

"Now we can start looking around for furniture," Liz said.

As she spoke, she wondered if Ike would be so tied up with the subway homicides that he wouldn't have time to shop. But he'd definitely stated he intended to have the case wrapped up by New Year's, she recalled.

If it turned out that way, they'd have plenty of time to find what they wanted before their mid-February wedding date.

Liz had just arrived at her desk, when she noticed several co-workers clustered around a workstation TV.

"Liz!" one of the women called. "It looks like the police got the subway killer!"

Liz rushed to turn on her own TV and caught the end of a bulletin saying the police had taken a man into custody. No further details were given.

Her co-workers filled her in. A man wearing a brown felt hat with a wide brim had been apprehended by police that morning on the Lexington Avenue local as it was pulling into the Twenty-eighth Street station. He had not been arrested but placed under temporary detainment and taken to a police station for questioning.

With the whole city now on the alert for a man wearing a hat of that description, Liz couldn't believe the killer would deliberately flaunt one on the very subway line where the murders had taken place.

At that moment she saw Dan entering his office and went to see if he'd heard the news. He had.

"I think this guy they got is some kind of a crank, or the cops would have arrested him," Dan said. "Evidently they didn't find any weapons or drugs on him, so they're just detaining him."

Liz nodded. Pop had told her about temporary detainment. The detainee can go free, under surveillance, until actually arrested, or he can remain in police custody till then.

"I heard that the man they picked up this morning chose to stay in custody," Dan continued. "That's unusual. It's as if he wants to be arrested."

Back at her desk, Liz found it difficult to concentrate on her work. She agreed with Dan—the man detained probably wasn't the killer. Most likely he was a harmless crank. But what if he wasn't harmless? What if he were planning a copycat killing?

During her first couple of hours at work, she was too busy to turn on her workstation TV and check for a news update on the fedora-flaunting detained man. When she was able to take a break, she found nothing on but a repeat of the original bulletin. If Ike had questioned the man, maybe he'd call her. She knew he wouldn't tell her much over the phone, but he might give her some idea of what was going on.

On her lunch break, she went with some co-workers to a grill in the vicinity, where a large-screen TV was always turned on. Although it was usually tuned to a sporting event, they felt sure this latest news about the crime spree that had gripped Manhattan for more than a week would supersede sports, at least for a while. Liz took her cell phone along and made sure it was on, so as not to miss a possible call from Ike.

Evidently the manager of the grill was as interested as they were in the arrest of a man wearing the highly publicized hat. The big-screen TV over the bar was on full blast, showing a male reporter conducting live, random street interviews—for lack of any real news about the man the police were detaining, Liz decided.

They settled themselves at a table just as the television

interviewer approached two young women coming out of a coffee shop and asked them for comments about the arrest of the man suspected of being the subway killer.

"I think it's him, all right, and he wanted to be caught," one woman replied. "If he didn't want to be caught, he wouldn't have put on his hat and gone back to the same subway where he killed those three women. It's like in a movie I saw once, where the murderer wrote a note saying, 'Please catch me before I kill again.'"

Her companion shook her head. "I don't believe this man is the killer. He's just someone who craves attention. When we get some more news about him, I'll bet it will come out that when they searched the place where he lives, they didn't find any needles or anything else suspicious."

The sound of her phone diverted Liz. She brought it out of her purse.

"Ike?"

"Yeah. I guess you caught the news that the cops picked up a man wearing an oversized fedora on the six train this morning."

"Right, I did. Have you questioned him?"

"Finished a little while ago. Where are you? Out eating lunch?"

"Yes—and watching TV. There's nothing new on about the man."

"Keep watching. Something should be coming on soon. Meanwhile, I might as well tell you what to expect."

Was he going to break his rule about never discussing his cases on the phone? she wondered. "What happened?" she asked.

She heard a note of annoyance in his voice. "He's been released. He made a phone call from the station house. Give a guess whom he called."

"Who? The mayor? Jesse Jackson? Hillary Clinton?"

"Very funny, but none of the above. He called the American Civil Liberties Union. He didn't even have to look up the number. He had it written down on a card in his pocket."

"Uh-oh. Is he going to claim his civil rights have been violated?"

"You got it. An attorney for the ACLU got over to the station house quicker than you could say, 'It's not against the law to wear a wide-brimmed fedora."

"But the cops didn't arrest him."

"Lucky they didn't. He was clean as a whistle."

"So the ACLU can't put together a case."

"They might try, but without an actual arrest, it won't jell. Under the circumstances, it's clear the cops were only doing their duty."

"With all the publicity, this guy must have known that a man wearing a hat like that was suspected of committing the subway murders, and that the police were looking for him," Liz said. "Yet he got on the six train wearing one. It's as if he deliberately set himself up."

"That's exactly what he did," Ike replied. "Like the cranks who confess to highly publicized murders they didn't commit, he wanted his day in the spotlight. What burns me up is the waste of time. We were diverted from the investigation to question this guy." He paused. "And

I'd just started looking into something on my own that I had to put on hold."

She knew he wasn't going to give her so much as a hint as to what he was looking into on his own. If he were going to tell her at all, he'd wait until they were together.

"I guess you're working late again tonight," she said.

"Yeah. I'm going to be tied up all evening. It doesn't look like we'll get to see each other at all. If it's not too late when I'm finished working, I'll phone you to say good night. Meanwhile, if you're interested in what the ACLU has to say about the crank in the fedora, there should be something on TV pretty soon."

After they said good-bye, Liz wondered what Ike could possibly be working on that would keep him tied up so late.

She and her co-workers finished lunch without seeing or hearing anything about the ACLU and the fedora crank. Back at her desk, Liz watched TV news for a few minutes, hoping to catch some coverage before she got to work. She was about to give up, when a commentator broke in.

"We interrupt this program to bring you a statement from a representative of the American Civil Liberties Union, concerning the man picked up by police this morning in connection with the subway homicides."

The ACLU spokesman came on. "An innocent man was apprehended by police today and hauled to a station house for no other reason than his wearing a fedora," he announced. "This is an outrage! Have we reached the point in this country where citizens are not free to wear the hats of their choice?"

Liz listened to his tirade for a few more moments before shaking her head and switching off the TV. The real outrage was the slowing down of a tough murder investigation to question a crackpot. With this thought she recalled Ike's saying that the time he'd spent questioning a crank had also kept him from looking into something on his own. She quelled her curiosity. Whatever it might be, she felt confident that he'd eventually let her in on it.

Chapter Twenty-five

Liz woke up the next morning knowing she wouldn't see Ike for the entire weekend. Late last night he'd called, saying he'd be working all day today and very late tonight and probably most of tomorrow.

"I'll miss you, Redlocks," he'd said. "But I'll make you a solemn promise. After this weekend, things will be better."

She'd never known Ike to make a promise he couldn't keep. "I'll miss you, too," she replied. She was going to say she hoped all this overtime meant he was close to solving the case, when he asked what she would be doing all weekend.

"How about going to Staten Island to see how Gram's new kitten is doing? Or getting together with Sophie?"

"Gram's off on a bus trip with her church friends, and I don't like to butt in on Sophie and Ralph's weekend. But I'm a big girl now. I'll find something to do.

Maybe I'll call one of my friends from work, or just stay put, catch up on my reading, watch some TV, and visit with Rosa and Joe. Rosa already invited me to eat Sunday dinner with them."

"Good. Sounds like you'll be okay."

He seemed very concerned about her weekend, she thought. "Of course I'll be okay," she said. "I hate not seeing you, but I'll be thinking about your promise."

"And don't forget, I'll phone you at four-thirty to-morrow."

"I'll be at the Moscarettis'. I'll be sure to take my cell."

Liz spent Saturday reading, watching TV, and visiting with Rosa and Joe.

The next day she and Rosa went to eleven o'clock mass. When they returned, Joe said he'd heard Liz's phone ringing.

"Whoever it was tried three times in the past ten minutes," he said.

Thinking of Pop and Mom, Liz hurried upstairs. They often called on Sunday, but always in the evening. It had to be something important to keep calling like that. There'd be a message on her answering machine.

She found three messages from Paula. In each of them she asked Liz to call back as soon as she got home. This was silly, Liz thought. One message would have been enough, but Paula was often silly. Something must have happened to upset her. Maybe the fancy house she wanted to buy had been snapped up by someone else, and she needed a shoulder to cry on. At that thought, Liz gave a sigh. The only shoulder available was hers.

She'd almost decided to ignore the phone calls— pretend she hadn't been home—but Paula would probably keep on calling and leaving more messages. She might as well call her and get it over with.

She was about to pick up the phone when Paula called again. "Hello, Liz. I'm glad I got hold of you at last." Her voice sounded troubled.

"Hi, Paula. I just got home from church. Is everything okay? Did you get the house you wanted?"

"Yes. That's one reason I called you—to tell you I made an offer on Friday, and it was accepted yesterday, and I've signed the contract. The house is vacant, and I was planning to move in next month."

"Paula, I can tell something's bothering you," Liz said.

"There is. That's the other reason I called you. It's Mr. Margolin."

"Your landlord? Has he been doing a lot of complaining about the barking?"

"Worse than that. Yesterday I gave him thirty days notice. When I said I was moving out in the middle of January, he told me I have to be out by Christmas!" Her voice rose to a wail. "That's less than two weeks away! How can I possibly move out before then?"

"I don't think he can do that to you," Liz said. "You have a lease, and you gave him notice. . . ."

"I can't stand hassling with him," Paula replied. "I'd rather just get out. But there's so much to do. I'm overwhelmed. I can probably line up a mover and schedule a date before Mr. Margolin's deadline, and the movers will come and do most of the packing, but that's the least of my worries. It's all the stuff I have to get rid of."

Liz asked herself what Paula would want to get rid of. Everything she'd seen in her apartment was either a priceless antique or brand-new from a pricey shop.

Paula must have sensed the question. "I'm getting a new bedspread made. The color won't go with the walls in my new house, and my towels won't look good with the tile in the new bathroom, so they'll have to go, too," she said. "And the lamps don't look right, either. And I'm getting all new cookware for my beautiful new kitchen. I want pots with copper bottoms so they'll look pretty hanging on the rack over the stove. And I'm replacing all my small appliances like my coffeemaker and food processor. All of them are white, and I want to get beige to match the kitchen cabinets. That's another reason I called you, Liz. Could you use my food processor? It's like new. I only used it once."

Liz tried not to picture herself with the food processor, whipping up goodies for Ike in Mr. Klein's vacated kitchen, but her efforts fizzled. The scene played out in her mind, and she could almost hear Ike telling her she was getting to be a great cook.

"Oh, thanks, Paula, I'd love to have it," she replied.

"Good. That's one thing I won't have to worry about. But what in the world am I going to do with all the other stuff? If there's anything else you want, Liz, please tell me. You're getting married soon, and you'll need things."

Liz resisted the temptation. "Thanks so much, but giving me the food processor is more than enough," she said. "And don't worry about getting rid of everything else. Some organization like the Salvation Army will take it all. Give them a call tomorrow."

Paula's voice sounded desperate. "It will be days before I can get everything all sorted and packed for pickup. I have to take it slow and easy. I've had a bad back ever since I was thrown from a horse when I was a kid. I had to give up riding and all other strenuous exercise. So I'll have to be careful, stooping and bending and lifting heavy things." She gave a deep sigh. "I'll never be able to get it all out of here before the deadline. I could leave it behind, but I'll be damned if I want Mr. Margolin to have it."

It might take Paula several days to sort and pack everything herself, Liz thought, and another few days for the Salvation Army to pick it up. Clearly, the time frame was too small. Paula needed help in packing her discards.

In spite of a little voice in her mind saying, *Don't do it,* Liz found herself rationalizing. She wouldn't see Ike all day. He said he'd call her at four-thirty this afternoon, but she might not see him until tomorrow. At least helping Paula would give her something to do this empty Sunday afternoon.

"I could come to pick up the food processor today and stick around to help you," she said. "I'm having four o'clock dinner with my neighbors, so I'll have to leave around three-thirty, but with the two of us working, we might be able to get it all packed, and you could call the Salvation Army tomorrow."

Paula's voice brightened. "Oh, Liz, would you really do that for me?"

Liz wasn't looking forward to another session of

Paula's nonstop chatter, but lending her a hand would help pass the time until Ike called.

"Yes," she replied. "Do you have enough boxes to hold all the giveaways?"

"Oh, yes—a bunch of them left over from when I moved here."

"Well, I'll get out of my church clothes and into my jeans and see you shortly," Liz said.

Paula's voice sounded happy. "Oh, thank you, thank you! You're a true-blue friend. While I'm waiting for you, I'll order us lunch from the caterer."

Dressed in designer jeans and shirt, Paula was waiting at the elevator. She gave Liz a hug, saying, "You're a real doll to help me out like this. Is your fiancé working overtime on the subway murders? Is that why you can spend this afternoon over here?"

"Yes, he's been very busy on the case," Liz replied.

"Lucky for me," Paula said with a laugh.

In her foyer, Brutus approached, growling, but in a moment he seemed to recognize Liz and didn't bark.

"See? He remembers you," Paula said. "Didn't I tell you he's smart?" She gave a sigh. "I wish he didn't hate cats. I miss having a cat, and I want to get one when I move. I know he'll bark a lot, but I can put up with it. At least I won't have to put up with Mr. Margolin."

She led the way into the kitchen, saying, "Before we get to work, let's have some lunch. They delivered it a few minutes ago."

She took a carton out of the refrigerator and arranged

the contents on two plates. "Shrimp salad," she said. "Shall we have some wine to go with it?"

"To celebrate your move away from Mr. Margolin? Sure!" Liz replied. She watched Paula remove a bottle from the temperature-controlled rack, uncork it, and pour the wine into two goblets.

At the table, Liz took a sip. "This is very good," she said.

"My ex-boyfriend introduced me to this wine," Paula replied, her voice suddenly sad. An instant later she put on a smile. "Don't worry, I'm not going to talk about him and go all weepy on you again," she added. "Let's talk about the latest development in the subway killings. How about that guy they picked up and let go? What did your fiancé have to say about him? Are they sure he isn't the killer?"

"They're sure. Ike says he deliberately wore a big fedora on the subway to get himself arrested and into the news," Liz replied.

"Well, he succeeded," Paula said. "He's been all over TV today, along with that fellow from the ACLU. Too bad. When I first heard about him on the news, I was sure they'd caught the killer." She shook her head. "I'll never understand what makes people like him tick. Didn't he realize pulling a stunt like that might hold up the murder investigation?"

"Most likely he's incapable of seeing beyond himself and doesn't give a damn about the investigation in progress," Liz replied.

A pensive look crossed Paula's face. "I'm probably being silly, but I keep thinking about Kyle and wondering if *he* should be investigated. That remark he made about my red hair sounded suspicious, don't you think?"

"Yes, it did." As Liz made the reply, a question popped into her mind: *Was it possible that the investigation Ike was doing on his own involved Paula's former paid escort?* That might account for his unusually heavy overtime.

Paula shuddered. "It makes me feel creepy, thinking I might have been paying a murderer to take me places. Let's not talk about him anymore."

They finished eating. Paula put the dishes and glasses into the dishwasher. "Are we ready to pack the giveaways?" she asked.

"The sooner we get to work, the sooner you can call the Salvation Army," Liz replied.

Paula led the way down the corridor off the foyer, opened the storeroom door, and switched on overhead lights. The room, lined on three walls with shelves, was crammed with all kinds of household furnishings.

"I know it's a mess in here with all the stuff I want to get rid of piled up on the floor," Paula said.

Liz, amazed by the number of articles Paula was disposing of, surveyed the heaps surrounding the packing boxes. "Don't worry, they'll soon be off the floor," she replied. "Looks like you have more than enough boxes."

Paula closed the door to keep Brutus out. "He curls up on anything soft and sheds hair all over it," she said.

They got to work. They wrapped wrong-color knick-knacks and other small breakables in newspaper and padded them with wrong-color ornamental bed pillows. With thick, plush, wrong-color towels and bath mats, they swathed framed paintings unworthy of Paula's new house. They put the unwanted cookware and other kitchen articles into the same box with wrong-color dish towels and table linens, leaving out only a few things for Paula to use until she moved and bought everything new.

By the time they'd filled three large boxes, there was still a good number of odds and ends remaining, and Paula said her back was starting to hurt.

Sitting down on a bench, also destined for the Salvation Army, Paula checked her watch. "It's after two-thirty," she said. "Let's take a break. I'm going to my room to lie down for a little while. I know you said you have to leave soon, and you probably want to keep on working, but if you're tired, you could go and stretch out on the living room couch."

Liz shook her head. "I'm not tired, and since I want to be on my way by three-thirty, I think I'll keep on working. I should be able to pack most of what's left before I have to leave."

"Okay," Paula said. "See you in about half an hour." She smiled over her shoulder as she closed the door. "Thanks so much, Liz."

Liz scrutinized the remainder of the discards. It wouldn't take her much more than half an hour to finish up, she decided. Paula shouldn't have to strain her back anymore today. She got to work, and it was only a quarter past three when she finished wrapping the last article—a silk lampshade, the wrong color for Paula's new bedroom.

Feeling pleased, she headed for the door, thinking

she'd take Paula up on the suggestion to relax on the living room sofa until it was time for her to leave.

When she couldn't open the door, she thought the lock must have sprung when Paula left the storeroom. After a few minutes of fiddling with the knob, she heard footsteps in the corridor.

"Paula? The door's stuck," she called.

"It does that sometimes," Paula replied. "I'll get it open."

Liz heard fumbling and scratching at the keyhole, then Paula's voice again. "It won't budge. I'll get the building superintendent."

While she was gone, Liz noticed that the door had inside hinges. If the super couldn't get the door open from the outside, she could remove the hinges herself. Surely there'd be a tool kit in the storeroom with a hammer and screwdrivers.

Paula was taking a long time to contact the super, she thought. Maybe he was off on Sundays and she was trying to get someone else.

"Paula!" she called. There was no response. Checking her watch, she knew if she didn't get out of there soon, she wouldn't make it to Rosa and Joe's in time for dinner. Her cell phone was in her purse on a table in the foyer. As soon as she could get to her cell phone, she'd call them and explain. But Ike had said he'd phone her around four-thirty, and there was no telling how long it would be before Paula returned. She might miss his call.

She'd adjusted herself to not seeing Ike all weekend. She'd counted on their telephone talks to ease the feeling of missing him. But now she was going to miss his phone call, and chances were, she wouldn't even hear his voice until tomorrow.

Suddenly, she eyed the door hinges and knew exactly what she was going to do. She'd take the bottom hinge off, pull the door open as far as it would go, squeeze through, and get to her cell phone. She'd call Rosa to say she might not make it for dinner. And she wouldn't miss Ike's call. If he phoned her apartment and couldn't reach her, he'd try her cell.

It didn't take her long to find a tool kit on one of the shelves. She took out a screwdriver and a light hammer and stuck them into her jeans pocket. As she closed the box, she noticed something behind it. Curious, she shoved the tool kit aside and found a brown coat and pants, neatly folded on the shelf. Why would Paula keep this in the storeroom instead of in her clothes closet? she wondered.

She unfolded the coat and held it up for further inspection. Paula would never wear anything like this masculine-looking, polyester pants suit, she thought, staring at it in puzzlement. Maybe it belonged to a former tenant. It should be packed with the other discards. Throwing the coat over her arm, she reached for the pants.

An instant later a cold chill raced down her spine. Farther back on the shelf, almost hidden in the shadows, was a wide-brimmed fedora!

Chapter Twenty-six

Liz stood there, numbed with shock and disbelief. But, incredible as it seemed, the truth was right in front of her eyes. It could not be denied. *Paula was the subway killer.*

How long she stared at the fedora, she would never remember. It could have been only a few minutes, or much longer, before her shattered senses cleared and she was able to fit the bits and pieces together.

Disguised as a man in the brown suit and fedora, Paula had jabbed three red-haired women with a toxic syringe. Now she'd locked another redhead in her storeroom and planned to kill her, too.

Little by little, she figured it all out.

Paula's former lover had not merely gone to work in California. Before he left, he'd dumped her for another woman who'd gone with him. And Liz had no doubts that the woman had red hair.

This was close to being Sophie's scenario: the insane grudge against redheaded women, the deranged desire to get even with them, and finally the crazed compulsion to kill them.

Had Paula dyed her hair in a desperate attempt to become a redhead and win back her lover before he left with her red-haired rival? Or had she done it to make sure she'd never be suspected of the killings she planned after he left her?

The answer lay in Paula's twisted mind.

Trying to detach herself from the horror and steel herself against the fear, she told herself she must stay calm. She must not allow herself to panic. That was her only chance of getting out of Paula's storeroom alive.

Why had Paula locked her in the storeroom? The answer was obvious: Paula was keeping her prospective victim locked up until the time was right to kill her. She'd been planning it from the moment she'd found out that her newfound, brown-haired friend was actually a strawberry blond. Her phone call today had been an elaborate ruse.

The thought crossed her mind that she should call for help. Maybe someone in a neighboring apartment would hear her. Mr. Margolin would certainly be at Paula's front door in a flash if he heard screams coming her apartment.

After reflecting on this, she shook her head. The storeroom was located on a short corridor between kitchen and foyer. It had no common walls with other apartments. Besides, if she called for help, Paula would hear her. She wanted to keep Paula away from the storeroom as long as possible. Also, she didn't want to risk having Paula suspect she'd found the fedora and figured everything out.

Was Paula planning to follow her usual MO and use a syringe filled with a lethal formula? Liz contemplated the answer calmly, as if the prospective victim were someone else. Yes, she decided. That method of murder was soundless and bloodless. If the grisly plan succeeded, Paula would bundle the body into one of the empty packing boxes. Then, on refuse collection day, the building superintendent would get it onto the freight elevator along with the rest of the trash.

But forewarned is forearmed, Liz told herself. She had an advantage. Paula didn't know her next intended victim had found the fedora and was wise to the subway killer. Most likely she was going to keep on playing the role of friend, pretending there was something wrong with the door lock, until she was ready for the kill. Then she'd "fix" the door and come into the storeroom. She'd think the lethal injection would be a piece of cake, because, like the subway victims, this one wouldn't be expecting an attack. Well, this redhead wasn't going to be jabbed to death without a fight!

Where was Paula? Of course she hadn't gone to find the superintendent. But she'd been gone for quite a while. Perhaps she was in her bathroom, mixing the deadly ingredients for the injection. Maybe it was taking longer than she expected. Maybe she'd discovered she was low on cyanide or something and was trying to figure out a substitute.

Suddenly Liz realized she still had the hammer and

screwdriver in her pocket. In her shock of finding out that Paula was the subway killer, removal of the door hinges had slipped her mind. She had wasted precious minutes. Was it too late to take the bottom hinge off before Paula came back? She had no choice. She had to try.

She thought of last summer, when she and Sophie had been locked in an abandoned icehouse. The door had had old-fashioned strap hinges on the inside. It had taken them many hours, but they'd managed to unscrew the two lower hinges with a small screwdriver Sophie had on her pocketknife. After a lot of pushing and pulling, they'd squeezed out through a very small opening. The thought cheered her. The hinges on that old, weathered door had been caked with century-old rust. This job should be easy by comparison.

Sophie would love hearing about this second round with door hinges, she thought, as she got to work with the hammer. And she *would* hear about it, she told herself firmly. She prayed that Paula wouldn't come back during the next ten minutes or so. That's all the time it should take for her to pop the bottom hinge. With a little finagling, she'd make enough room to wriggle through, then sprint down the corridor to the foyer where she'd left her coat and her purse containing her cell phone.

But the job was barely started when she felt her heart sink. She heard footsteps approaching in the corridor, followed by Paula's voice calling, "What's that banging?" She sounded annoyed, almost angry, Liz thought.

She should have known Paula would hear the hammering, but why was she so annoyed? Liz wondered.

Maybe her speculations about Paula's lengthy absence had been right on the mark. Maybe she *had* run out of some poisonous component and had to alter the formula with household bleach or something. That could have made her grouchy.

Paula's voice sounded again, closer to the door. "Did you hear me, Liz?"

Liz did some rapid thinking before replying. Paula wasn't aware she'd found the fedora and knew who the killer was. She wouldn't realize removing the door hinges was an attempt to escape becoming the fourth red-haired victim. There was still a chance she could bluff her way out of this.

"You were gone so long, I was getting claustrophobic in here," she said. "I started to take the door off the hinges so I could get out."

The instant the words were spoken, Liz realized she'd made a big mistake. Paula now knew she'd removed a hammer from the toolbox on the shelf. It wouldn't take her long to figure out she'd seen what was behind it. With her heart pounding, Liz waited.

For a moment, all was silent on the other side of the door. Then Paula's voice came, no longer annoyed but almost gentle.

"You know, don't you?"

Liz felt a clutch of fear at her heart. Again, she heard Paula's voice.

"I'm sorry it has to be this way, Liz. I liked you. I really did."

Along with Liz's fear came a chilling realization: *It wasn't the hammering that had brought Paula to the storeroom door. She had the loaded syringe with her. She was ready to rid the world of one more redhead.*

Liz knew that time was running out. At any moment now she'd hear Paula getting the key from above the door. . . .

With her heart pounding, she looked around for something she could use to defend herself. If only the hammer in her hand were not so small. And if only Brutus would start barking. That would divert Paula and bring an irate Mr. Margolin to the apartment. She could call out to him for help.

With this thought, an idea flashed into her mind. It was a long shot, but it just might work. Stepping close to the door, praying that Mr. Margolin was at home, and thinking of Gram's old Hercules, she summoned the full strength of her vocal chords.

"Mmmerrrow! Mmmerrrow!"

Barks sounded from somewhere in the apartment. Encouraged, she tried again.

"Mmmerrrow!"

Paula must have figured out what she was trying to do. "Stop that!" she exclaimed. Liz could hear her fumbling for the key. But it was too late. Brutus was at the storeroom door, baying like a hound in hot pursuit of quarry.

She heard Paula scuffling with him, trying to subdue him and get him away from the door. "Brutus! Quiet! Bad dog!"

To keep the din at top level, Liz let out a few more catcalls. The barking continued, unabated.

Above the noise, she heard the sound of the doorbell,

and Paula's footsteps going to answer it. *It had to be Mr. Margolin.* She breathed a prayer of thanks.

Paula's voice drifted down the corridor, almost drowned out by Brutus, but there was no doubt she was talking to someone. Liz knew that Paula would try to keep Mr. Margolin from stepping into the foyer, where he would be more likely to hear calls for help. She thought of trying to finish removing the bottom hinge from the door but decided it would take too long. By the time she was able squeeze out and run to the foyer, Mr. Margolin might have left. She might come face-to-face with Paula in the corridor.

She pictured Paula coming at her with a deadly syringe. There'd be a struggle. Even if she gave it all she had, the odds were against her. Paula was taller and heavier. Her best chance would be to call out to Mr. Margolin—*now.*

Standing close to the door, she shouted with every bit of strength she had in her.

"Mr. Margolin! Mr. Margolin! Mr. Margolin!"

Would her voice be lost in the wild barking?

Her heart bounded with hope when she heard footsteps coming down the corridor. Voices, blending with barks, sounded closer, until she sensed that Paula and Mr. Margolin were just outside the storeroom door.

With no more catcalls emanating from the storeroom, Brutus suddenly stopped barking. She almost wept with joy and relief when she heard a man's voice clearly.

"No, I was not mistaken, Ms. Rubik. That's no radio in your storeroom. I distinctly heard someone call my name."

240 *Dorothy P. O'Neill*

Liz's spirits rose with her voice. "Please help me, Mr. Margolin!" she called. "Ms. Rubik locked me in here. She—"

But as quickly as her spirits had risen, they plummeted when Paula interrupted, her voice calm and convincing, speaking over the explanation Liz would have made.

"I hoped I wouldn't have to tell you this, Mr. Margolin. It's painful and upsetting—but that's my sister in there. She has a mental illness, and if she doesn't take her medication, she becomes delusional and sometimes violent. I had to confine her when she told me she knew I was going to kill her and she started hitting me. That's why my dog was barking. He's very protective of me."

Liz's spirits reached their lowest ebb. Anything she'd say now would back Paula up one hundred percent. But she had to make an attempt. She spoke rapidly, trying to say as much as she could before Paula broke in with more lies, but being careful not to mention that Paula was the subway killer. That would only make Mr. Margolin believe Paula.

"She's lying, Mr. Margolin. I'm not her sister, and she's the one with the mental illness—not me. She locked me in here, and she's holding me against my will. The key's over the door. Please, let me out, and I'll explain everything."

She knew that even this watered-down version of the truth had made Mr. Margolin decide she was, indeed, mentally ill when he responded not to her but to Paula. "Are you sure you can handle this? Your sister sounds as if she should be in an institution."

"I know what to do when she gets like this," came the glib reply. "She'll be all right when I get her calmed down and see that she takes her pills. She came from Oklahoma to visit me for Christmas, and the hassles in the airports and the time change must have thrown her off schedule."

Evidently Margolin believed her. His voice sounded as if he'd turned away from the door. "Well, all right, but I'm telling you again, Ms. Rubik, if you don't keep that dog quiet, I'm going to call the police, and you'll be fined for disturbing the peace," he said. "You're only going to be here till the middle of next month, but during that time I'm not going to put up with it. Several tenants have already complained."

. . . only going to be here till the middle of next month! Liz realized that Paula had lied about Mr. Margolin's pre-Christmas deadline. It had been part of the plan to get her over here and into the storeroom.

To her dismay, she heard their footsteps retreating. Mr. Margolin was on his way back to the foyer. She couldn't let him leave without trying to convince him that Paula was lying. His mention of the police gave her an idea.

"Please, Mr. Margolin!" she called, trying to sound the direct opposite of a violent, delusional woman. "If you have a phone on you, please call the police immediately and report that a woman is being held here against her will."

She longed to mention the subway homicides but thought it would sound much too delusional. Being held against her will sounded a little less crazy. She had to stick to that and hope it would work.

He made no reply, but she heard Paula's voice. "Poor sis. She really needs her pills."

She sounded as if they were halfway up the corridor. Another minute and they'd be in the foyer, and then Mr. Margolin would be gone, along with her last chance.

In desperation, she shouted after them. "Mr. Margolin! Please, *please* call the police in this precinct and report this!" An idea flashed into her mind, and she added, "Ask the officer who takes your call to contact Detective George Eichle."

She did not want to say anything more. It might make her sound even crazier than Mr. Margolin thought she was.

She put her ear against the door and strained to hear whatever reply or comment Mr. Margolin might make. When it came, it was barely audible, but it was clear enough for her to know her last chance was gone.

"I hope you can get your sister calmed down, Ms. Rubik."

And then came the sound of a door closing.

Chapter Twenty-seven

In despair, Liz sank to the floor and covered her face with her hands, telling herself she should have pulled out all the stops. She should have yelled something about the subway homicides at the top of her lungs. Mr. Margolin hadn't believed her restrained story, anyway. A more startling one might have given him something to think about.

Now all she could do was wait for Paula to come back. But she wasn't going to wait here on the floor like some sniveling weakling, she decided. She got to her feet and listened at the door. She heard no footsteps. Why hadn't Paula come rushing down the corridor in triumph, ready to get on with her grisly plan?

Liz felt sure Paula had the loaded syringe on her when she'd asked that chilling question outside the storeroom door. She could still hear those words. *"You know, don't you?"*

Maybe on her way to the door to confront Mr. Margolin, she'd stashed the syringe. There wouldn't have been room for it in a pocket of her tight, designer jeans, and she certainly wouldn't want him to see it. She was probably getting it out of its hiding place now, and she'd be back here at any moment.

Sure enough, a few minutes later she heard footsteps in the corridor. She braced herself for what was to come and told herself again that Paula was going to be in for one hell of a fight from this scrappy little Irish redhead. But Paula was about four inches taller and more than a few pounds heavier. With such an advantage, could she possibly be overpowered? Recalling that Paula had a bad back, her spirits rose, only to sag again with the thought that this, too, was probably part of Paula's elaborate ruse. Her back was hurting, she'd said, and she'd gone, supposedly to lie down, after locking her intended victim in the storeroom.

Now Paula's voice came through the door. "You thought you were pretty smart, didn't you? Well, that cat trick won't work again. I shut Brutus in my bedroom with the TV on. He couldn't hear you if you tried."

Liz remembered what Paula had said, right after she'd asked, *"You know, don't you?"*

"I'm sorry it has to be this way, Liz. I liked you. I really did."

She thought the words might indicate that some small part of Paula was capable of normal, human emotions. Perhaps there was a chance of reasoning with her and persuading her to give herself up.

"Paula," she said. "You told me you were sorry about

this, and you said you liked me. Can't we talk about this, as friends?"

"There's nothing we can talk about anymore," Paula replied. "You're a red-haired woman. You're all alike."

Liz hadn't really expected a "yes." In her heart she knew that kind of storybook happy ending was not going to happen. She'd reached the stage where she was clutching at straws. Now she knew she had to stop dreaming and look for something to whack Paula over the head with the instant she stepped into the storeroom. Would the very small hammer in her pocket possibly knock Paula out? She couldn't risk botching it. Then she remembered she'd seen a larger hammer in the toolbox.

But why hadn't Paula come into the storeroom yet? Why was she hanging around in the corridor? She'd been out there for ten or fifteen minutes. Why didn't she unlock the door and get on with her murderous plan?

Paula's next words provided the answer. "I had you fooled, didn't I?" she asked. "And you really went for that remark I told you Kyle made, didn't you? I almost laughed in your face when I was telling you I thought he might be the subway killer."

Paula was enjoying this, Liz thought. She was in no hurry. It was as if she were a cat playing with a mouse until she was ready for the kill.

"I have to admit, you had me worried for a couple of minutes when you were begging old Margolin to call the police," Paula went on. "But the more you said, the loonier you sounded." She laughed. "You should have seen his face!"

While Paula talked on, taunting her, Liz went to the toolbox and took the larger hammer out and slid it into her pants pocket. It was the best she could come up with. She prayed she could get in a swift blow to the head when Paula finally opened the door. With a lot of strength and a little luck, that first blow might crush her skull.

The thought made her shudder. But this was no time to be squeamish. If she didn't bring that hammer down as hard as she could, Paula's head might only be grazed. Paula could counter by jabbing the needle right then and there.

A sense of unreality came over her. It was hard to believe that the friendship Paula seemed to want had developed into a deadly contest. Little more than an hour ago Paula's constant chatter had annoyed her. Now she wished the taunting talk would never end.

For now, it showed no signs of letting up. "I guess your detective fiancé is searching for a fedora in the homes and business offices of the baker and his twin sister, and the doctor and the pest-control guy, and the rest of them," Paula said. "He can't be much of a detective if he hasn't suspected by this time that the subway killer could be someone with no connection at all to those dead redheads."

Liz wanted to scream at her, saying that Ike was known as one of the best detectives in all of Manhattan, but at that moment she realized Paula had finally stopped talking. In the sudden quiet, Liz heard a brushing sound— Paula's hands groping for the key above the door. She took the hammer out of her pocket and waited, trembling, for the scrape of the key in the lock.

But instead of that, the next sound she heard sent her fearful heart into a joyful spin—a loud knock on the apartment door, followed by an authoritative voice.

"Police! Open up!"

There could be only one explanation. *Mr. Margolin must have called the precinct after all.*

She heard Paula's footsteps running up the corridor to the foyer. Was she going to stash the syringe and try to talk her way out of this? An uneasy feeling dulled her bright spirits. Mindful of the convincing story Paula had devised before, she felt strong misgivings.

She heard another knock, then Paula's voice. "All *right,* I'm coming." Then the sound of the apartment door opening and closing, and voices in the foyer.

What if this became an instant replay? No one knew better than she how convincing Paula could be. What if she were telling the cops that Mr. Margolin had overreacted, and they believed her?

The possibility threw her into a belated panic. She found herself pounding on the storeroom door with the hammer. She heard her own voice screaming, "Please, please, don't believe her! She locked me in the storeroom! The key's over the door! Please, help me!"

Even in her panic, she thought if she cried out that Paula was the subway killer, this would only reaffirm Paula's lies.

A moment later she heard what sounded like the apartment door being opened. She'd believed her spirits had already hit rock bottom, but now they fell to new depths of despair. The cops must not have heard her calls for help. Whatever Paula had told them, they'd believed her, and now they were leaving.

The strain of the past hour's ordeal, the change in her spirits again and again from thankful high to fearful low, now began to take its toll. She felt the sting of tears on her face. Hoping the cops would hear her before the door closed behind them, she summoned every bit of strength she had and gave it one last try. Surely there would be some response to her repeated pleas.

"Please, please help me!" she called. "Don't leave me here!"

But all she heard was the sound of the apartment door closing.

Chapter Twenty-eight

B ut in the next instant she heard the sound of someone running down the corridor, and a voice that turned
her despairing tears into tears of joy.

"Hang in there, Redlocks!"

She heard the key in the lock, and seconds later she
was in Ike's arms. He drew her to the bench, folded her
into his arms, and gently kissed her face, still traced with
tears.

"It's okay now," he said, holding her trembling body
close to his.

With her heart racing and her mind still mired in the
aftermath of her ordeal, she could only cling to him,
whispering, "I . . . I thought the cops had left. I heard
the door . . ."

"That was me, coming in," he said. "I got here a few
minutes after the uniforms and found them trying to
subdue Paula."

"Subdue her?" Liz's mind cleared. She pictured Paula in a struggle with the cops.

"Yeah. They said they heard someone banging on a door and calling for help, and when they told Paula they were going to search the apartment, she went berserk. It took the two of them to get her under control."

Within the comfort of his arms, her heart slowed its pace, her dreadful feelings ebbed, and her voice steadied. "When they didn't answer my calls for help, I thought Paula had talked her way out of this."

"They said she tried, but since they were responding to a report from a Mr. Margolin that a woman was being held against her will at this address, and that she'd mentioned my name, it didn't work."

Now Liz put it all together. Mr. Margolin not only called the police but remembered to ask the officer who took the call to notify Detective George Eichle.

"I had no idea who Mr. Margolin was, except he was the landlord of the building where the woman was being held," Ike continued. "But when I got this address, I recognized it as Paula's, and I knew right away that the woman being held was you. He paused to give her a gentle kiss. "Thank God you're okay. The uniforms have probably taken her in by now. She'll be booked for crimes against persons."

Liz stared at him in shocked disbelief. "No!" she exclaimed. "It's much more than that. Please don't think this has driven me out of my mind, Ike, but I know Paula is the subway killer!"

"Simmer down, Redlocks," he said. "I know she's the subway killer, but she has to be charged with something else until we can get hold of some hard evidence to make it homicide."

Relief flooded over her, calming her agitation. "I have the evidence—but how did you know she's the killer?"

"It's a long story. First I have to make some calls, and then I need to hear your full account of what happened and have a look at whatever evidence you have."

He gave her a quick kiss, got to his feet, and took his phone out of his pocket.

By now she felt almost normal. "While you're making your calls, I need to call Rosa," she said. "But my phone's on the foyer . . ." She glanced toward the door. "Is Paula still out there with the cops? I don't want to see her."

"I'll go with you and make my calls from the living room," Ike replied. "Don't worry about encountering Paula. By now she should be on her way to jail."

The foyer was empty. Liz called Rosa and told her she couldn't make it for dinner. "I'll explain when I see you, tonight or tomorrow," she said.

Meanwhile, Ike called his partner and his squad lieutenant, and left a message for the district attorney. "I'm going to his office with this first thing tomorrow," he reported. "Now, do you feel up to giving me your full statement?"

She told him everything. "The fedora and the man's suit are on a shelf in the storeroom," she said. She glanced around the living room. "But that's not all the evidence. I'm pretty sure Paula stashed a loaded syringe in here somewhere."

"Good. Let's look for it before we go back to the storeroom."

It didn't take them long to find the needle behind a sofa pillow. They left it there to be bagged and then went back to the storeroom.

She led him to the shelf where the fedora lay behind the toolbox, and the mannish suit where she'd dropped it in shocked realization. He eyed it all with a pleased grin, saying, "Lou and some uniforms are on their way here. They'll get shots of the evidence before it's bagged."

"I know now, this is what you've been investigating on your own," she said. "What gave you the idea that Paula might be the subway killer?"

He motioned toward the bench. "Let's sit down. Like I said, it's a long story."

He began by saying he'd talked to the man from the escort service. "First, I asked him a few questions about Paula, and he said she always talked a lot about herself and her rich family. She also told him she had a degree in veterinary medicine. He was surprised when I asked him about the remark she said he'd made concerning her red hair. Of course he denied it, and I got the feeling he wasn't lying."

"He wasn't," Liz said. "After Paula had me locked in here, she told me she'd made that up."

"She made up having a veterinarian's degree, too," Ike replied. "I contacted Dr. Jurgens at her home, and she told me Paula doesn't have any training whatsoever in that field. Dr. Jurgens said she hired her because of her fondness for animals and she noticed that animals responded to her. Also, her first impression was that Paula had a warm personality that would be helpful in dealing with anxious pet owners."

Liz nodded, recalling her first impression of Paula.

"But get this," Ike continued. "The doctor said that Paula's warm personality didn't wear well. 'She came on too strong,' was how she put it."

"I know exactly what she meant," Liz said. "What else did you find out?"

"Remember when you told me about Paula's skull-cap?"

"Yes . . ."

"At the time the thought occurred to me that a skull-cap is often used as part of a disguise, including makeup and a mustache or beard. I didn't connect Paula with this, and I forgot about it until after I talked with the escort guy and the veterinarian. With this in mind, I decided to question the night doorman at her apartment building. I made it seem as if the questioning was part of a police effort to protect red-haired women who live in the vicinity of the Lex local."

"You never cease to amaze me," Liz said.

"Thanks. The results of my questions were pretty amazing, too. When I asked the night doorman if Ms. Rubik often went out at night alone, he said he was new on the job, but he recalled she'd gone out alone last Wednesday night. She'd left the building soon after she'd gotten home from work, he said."

"Last Wednesday night? That's when the fedora man tried to needle another redhead near Rockefeller Center!"

"Yeah, and there's more. The doorman said when she went out that night, he noticed she wasn't dressed in her usual style. 'Miss Rubik is a snappy dresser,' was how he put it, but that night she was wearing a baggy brown pants suit and a scarf over her head."

"Wow!" Liz exclaimed.

"I talked with the day doorman, too," Ike continued. "He remembered her leaving the building earlier than usual several mornings, wearing a brown pants suit and head scarf. He couldn't recall exactly which mornings, but he remembered thinking it was strange when she came back later and then left for her job dressed in different clothing. By that time I was beginning to sense something fishy about Paula."

Liz turned this over in her mind and formed her own scenario. On Wednesday night, Paula had left her apartment building with the fedora concealed under the baggy suit coat. In a ladies' room somewhere in Rockefeller Center, she'd put on dark makeup and a mustache, switched from scarf to fedora, and gone out to look for another redhead.

When she ran this by Ike, he nodded. "I'm sure, now, that's what she did. And she followed the same procedure in the subway restrooms. Her work hours gave her enough time to get home, change into her disguise, and board the subway during evening rush hours. During the morning rush hours, she had time to ride the subway, looking for victims, and then go back to her apartment to get ready for work."

"Wouldn't all that have been enough to make Paula a suspect?" Liz asked.

He shook his head. "It was all conjecture. Before I took it to the DA, I had to get something more. I thought if I could locate the former night doorman, and he recalled

Paula's going out after work dressed in that baggy suit, it would help. I also thought a thorough background check on Paula might uncover something incriminating. I figured if her family is as wealthy as she says, I could look them up on the Internet."

"Did you find the Rubiks on the Internet, and are they loaded?" Liz asked.

"Yeah. That was the only thing she didn't lie about. I got the name of a town in Oklahoma. Seems the Rubiks own most of it. It wasn't hard to contact relatives, and through them, schoolteachers. With the time difference between here and Oklahoma, I was able to work on it after my regular hours. Between the Internet and the telephone, I got plenty of information from relatives and schoolteachers, none of it favorable to Paula."

"Like what?" Liz asked.

"According to some surprisingly frank statements, she's an inveterate liar with an extremely jealous nature. Because of this, she was unable to form any lasting friendships. Even though she was very pretty, and boys were attracted to her at first, she couldn't hang on to any boyfriends."

"That would explain why her romance in New York fizzled," Liz said.

"Yeah, and get this. She was suspected of tampering with the stirrups of another girl's horse before a horse show because she thought the girl would win the blue ribbon she wanted. The girl was thrown and severely injured. Paula had been seen loitering around the horse's stall just before the show started. But there was no proof, so she got away with it."

"All that sounds like evidence," Liz said. "Couldn't you have acted on it?"

Ike shook his head. "It's valuable information, but by itself, it's hearsay. I needed more. I knew I had to find the former night doorman. If he remembered Paula's leaving the building on a definite evening, wearing the outfit the other two doormen described, I thought the DA would go for a case against Paula."

"Why didn't you tell me about all this?"

"It all seemed too bizarre to be for real, and I knew you were trying to keep your wildfire imagination in check, but I planned to let you in on it as soon as I got a statement from the former doorman."

"Were you able to locate him?"

"Yeah. I met with him this afternoon, and what he had to say backed up what the other two told me. He definitely remembered Paula's wearing the mannish suit and a scarf over her head on one of those unusually warm evenings. He recalled thinking it was strange. The outfit wasn't stylish, like she usually wore, and also the suit was too heavy for such warm weather. This was enough for me to take to the DA, but he was away over the weekend. I didn't want to run it by an assistant, so I decided to hold off until Monday morning."

He paused, looking at her with obvious regret. "I shouldn't have held off. But most of all, I should have told you I suspected Paula. If I hadn't dragged my feet, you wouldn't have—"

She silenced him with a kiss. "Don't beat yourself up. Last time we talked on the phone, neither of us had the slightest idea that Paula would get me over here today."

"Yeah, you assured me you were going to spend a quiet Sunday at home and have dinner with Rosa and Joe, and I told you I'd call you at four-thirty. I figured I'd be through interviewing the doorman by then."

Again, he told her he should have warned her to stay away from Paula. "Thank God I was in the station house when Margolin called."

"And thank God when I was screaming at him to help me, I mentioned your name."

"Yeah. He told the officer he almost didn't make the call, but he got thinking, how would a woman visiting from Oklahoma know the name of an NYPD detective?"

At that moment an ear-piercing sound came from somewhere down the hall. It was howling, growling, and barking, all put together.

"What the hell was that?" Ike asked.

"It's Paula's dog, Brutus. She locked him in her bedroom so he wouldn't bark if I tried to get Mr. Margolin over here again by meowing like a cat."

Ike looked puzzled for a moment before breaking into a grin. "I think I get it. Paula told you that Margolin was always complaining about her dog's barking, and you figured a few catcalls would get him going again, and when Margolin came to complain, you'd be home free."

"Right. It didn't go as I planned, but the end result was exactly what I wanted. I wish you could have heard me. I did my imitation of Gram's old cat, Hercules."

He drew her into a hug. "Those catcalls and barks are directly responsible for solving the most baffling murder case New York has had in many years."

"I can see the headlines in the *Post*," she said. "Pets Put Paula in Pen."

"Or, Sleuth's Sweetie Nabs Subway Syringer," he replied with a laugh. "You did it, Liz."

"Thanks, but you had it figured out, and you were ready to move on Paula."

He tightened his arms around her. " 'Ready' wouldn't hack it. I could have lost you."

Just then a knock at the apartment door told them Ike's partner had arrived with the uniformed officers. When Ike let them in, loud barks sounded from the bedroom.

One of the cops, a young man Liz judged to be in his midtwenties, looked concerned. "A dog," he said. "What's going to happen to it?"

Evidently the word was out, Liz thought. After the arresting officers had taken Paula to the station house, Ike had been called with the news that the charges against her would be changed to homicide—specifically, the subway murders. As an alleged serial killer, most likely Paula would not get bail. She'd be locked up, tried, and convicted. Brutus would never see her again.

"Poor Brutus—I don't know what will happen to him," Liz replied.

"After we're done, I'd like to have a look at him," the officer said.

While the initial evidence was being photographed and bagged, a search of Paula's bathroom turned up more syringes and some vials of lethal material. Pending analysis, the material was believed to be chloral hydrate and hydrogen cyanide—swiped from Dr. Jurgens' supply cabinet, Liz felt sure.

She figured that none of Dr. Jurgens' staff had been suspected of the theft because of similar break-ins at other veterinarians' offices. And Paula had smashed the ground-floor window to make sure the police would call it an outside job.

By the time the cops were ready to leave the apartment, the young officer who'd inquired about Brutus had become acquainted with him and now had him on a leash.

"This dog might be a good candidate for the K-9's," he said with a broad smile. "But if he doesn't make it, I've always wanted a Doberman."

Chapter Twenty-nine

Walking from the apartment building to Ike's Taurus, Ike asked Liz if she wanted to go somewhere to eat. "I'm hungry," he said. "I was too busy earlier to get around to lunch."

Liz looked down at her rumpled jeans and shirt. "I'm not exactly dressed for fine dining. How about takeout at my place?"

The instant she asked, she thought of Rosa and Joe. They'd be out of their apartment before she and Ike could hit the stairs, wanting to know why she couldn't make it to dinner with them. Much as she loved them, she didn't feel up to explanations tonight. She'd tell them everything tomorrow.

"On second thought, could we have takeout at your place instead of mine?" she asked.

She could tell by his smile, he understood.

"Sure," he replied.

They picked up burgers and fries and drove to Ike's apartment, downtown near the Battery. She'd been there a few times; thus, she was prepared for a bachelor pad that bore no resemblance to those depicted in old movies starring Carry Grant.

Ike carried the food through the living room, furnished only with a sofa, a chair, a TV, and an untidy computer desk, into a small kitchen containing a table with two mismatched chairs.

"I need to get cleaned up," Liz said, heading for the pink-tiled bathroom with the green shower curtain and the blue towels.

"I'll get the plates out, and I'll have the wine poured by the time you get back," he replied.

Looking into the mirror on the medicine cabinet over the sink, Liz was not surprised that she looked disheveled after what she'd been through. But better disheveled than dead, she thought.

Back in the kitchen, Ike handed her a glass of wine. "Here's to your catcalling skills," he said.

They touched glasses. Liz took a sip before raising her glass again. "Here's to Brutus," she said. "And let's not forget Mr. Margolin."

"And a special toast to the end of the subway homicides case," Ike added.

They touched glasses again, and Liz said she had another. "To the end of my brown hair."

"Yeah, in a few weeks, maybe," Ike replied. "I want my red-haired sweetheart back. How long will it take to fade?"

"I'm not waiting," Liz said, as they sat down to eat.

"Gram says there's something that takes the color out right away. If you'll stop at a drugstore when you drive me home, I'll buy it and use it tonight. Next time you see me, I'll be back to normal."

Ike smiled. "And so will our life. It's a great feeling, knowing it's all over. Now I know you'll be Redlocks on our wedding day and forever after."

"You won't be calling me Redlocks on our golden anniversary," she said with a laugh. "If I'm still into sleuthing fifty years from now, you'll have to change it to Graylocks."

He reached across the table, clasped her hand, and looked into her eyes, saying, "Whether or not you're still into sleuthing after fifty years, you'll always be Redlocks to me."